"In one of Chekhov's stories, a character says that every happy man should have someone who taps at his door with a little hammer, reminding him that there are unhappy people in the world. Reading Celeste Mohammed's novel-in-stories makes me think of that magical little tap—except that the door opens not to a vision of unhappiness, but to a world crammed with life that you never knew existed."
—CLAIRE ADAM, author of *The Golden Child*

"As James Joyce did for Dublin, Celeste Mohammed holds up a polished mirror to the inhabitants of the fictitious Trinidadian town of Pleasantview and dares the reader to take an unflinching look at a multi-ethnic society that is vibrant and joyous but riddled with corruption and the exploitation of women, the young, and the vulnerable. Mohammed's writing is smart, funny, and enlivened by everyday Trinidadian vernacular, creating rich and lively portraits of a range of Trini characters. A formidable debut, *Pleasantview's* razor-sharp observations of misogyny and the abuse of power are leavened by humor and a pitch-perfect ear for the language of human foibles."
—TONY EPRILE, author of *The Persistence of Memory*

"*Pleasantview* offers the reader a sharp and fearless view of the dark underbelly of life in Trinidad, filled with unforgettable characters that we meet in do-or-die situations. Marked by male violence, political underhandedness, and economic desperation, *Pleasantview* also demonstrates Mohammed's remarkable range as a v   ousness to tenderness,   in a work that lingers in the reader's mind long after the final page. This is a thrilling debut."

—**LAURIE FOOS**, author of *Ex Utero* and *The Blue Girl*

"The residents of the fictional Trinidadian town of Pleasantview are divided by mistrust and racial and ethnic tension, but they are forever bound to each other by their shared histories and secrets. From Omar who is forced to confront his boss's corruption, to Miss Ivy in her employer's hand-me-down fur coat outside the police station, Mohammed's characters demand to be acknowledged. In this beautifully written debut, Mohammed gives voice to the silenced and the overlooked. *Pleasantview* sizzles with originality and heart and introduces a fearless new writer."

—**HESTER KAPLAN,** author of *Unravished*

"Celeste Mohammed forces you to travel with her characters. You see their lives and their world as they do, on foot. You walk in her characters' shoes. Mohammed is a skillful storyteller, so the journey educates and exhilarates you, Mohammed invents a clear, crackling town/district, Pleasantview, a bustling, hustling side of Trinidad, where few of us have ever been, or will ever go. *Pleasantview* forces us to look at how we behave when uncontained, when unconstrained, when our lack of morality unmoors us."

—**A.J. VERDELLE**, author of *The Good Negress*

Pleasantview

Pleasantview

Celeste Mohammed

NEW YORK, NY

Printed in the United States of America.
10 9 8 7 6 5 4 3 2 1

Ig Publishing
Box 2547
New York, NY 10163

www.igpub.com

ISBN: 978-1-63246-202-2

For Sarai Ayesha

❀ CONTENTS ❀

Foreword

In 1959, a little-known street in Trinidad, located in one of the poorer areas inhabited by Indo-Trinidadians, was brought to life by the writer V.S. Naipaul. In his collection, *Miguel Street*, Naipaul used candor and humor to write about a cast of improbable characters whose stories reflected the lives of ordinary people. This early collection of short stories would establish Naipaul's extraordinary voice on the horizon of English language.

"I rather suspect the mantle of Chekhov has fallen on Mr. Naipaul's shoulders" wrote a reviewer of the collection, Robert Payne.

Trinidadians are natural storytellers. Back in the early 1930s, *The Beacon* magazine opened the literary floodgates to pioneering local voices. Read C.L.R. James, Arthur Mendes, Michael Anthony, Earl Lovelace. Listen to Trinidad's calypsos. Stories evoking place and character, then reflecting the issues of a British colony; voices that longed to set their island free.

Seventy years later, here we are in Pleasantview, again in one of the poorer areas of this now-independent island nation, inhabited by modern day Trinidadians whose daily dramas may differ from those of decades ago, but whose basic concerns of poverty, violence, misogynism, sexuality, religion, education, politics, crime, love and betrayal, remain universal.

In a now-established literary tradition, the versatility of Celeste Mohammed's voice is evident not just in her use of the various accents and quirks of dialogue that provide authenticity and individuality, but in the fluidity of her point of view as it shifts from omniscient author to that of her characters, male and female, so that we too inhabit their lives. So the reader is there with a bird's-eye view at times and then has the immediacy of dipping into the character's thought at others. The effect is that of a camera taking long aerial shots and then zooming in, allowing us glimpses of intimacy and insight we would otherwise only be able to guess at.

Each story in *Pleasantview* is a strand of a tapestry. As the characters step forward one by one, we get a sense of who they are and how they relate to each other, until we are presented with a whole village—from the emotionally bankrupt Mr. Jagroop, to the doomed Sunil and Consuela; Jagroop's young tenant Omar, who struggles to defend his values; and Gail, who turns to the village soothsayer with her own history of his abuse after she falls victim to the despicable Mr. H, the ruthless shopkeeper and deceitful husband. The tangled web of village and family relationships is revealed by Kimberley, who escapes her father's reach and tries to find herself in probably the most intricately woven and moving of the stories; the cultist clutch of the church on Michelle's spirit which abandons the "hell" in Michelle to turn into Ruth, who becomes a stranger to her husband Declan. The lure of America as an economic salve splits up a family— Judith and Luther—which has far-reaching consequences for each and for their marriage, and when their vulnerable son Jason seeks his own life's answers.

This collection could well have been subtitled "Santimanitay," for the stories are truly tales that turn the everyday life of the ironically named Pleasantview inside out, exposing truth "without mercy." This collection announces an uncommon voice and a rich talent. It also reveals that the dynamics of poverty, human joy, human misery, the effect of love on the heart, the cruelty of power, the often misguided need for identity and comfort, the high price paid for secrecy, remain very much the same today as they always were.

It's my turn to suspect the mantle of Chekov, then Naipaul, has now fallen to Celeste Mohammed.

—Rachel Manley

Prologue: The Dragon's Mouth (Bocas del Dragón)[1]

IT HAVE A BENEFIT TO BEING on this prison island, this tiny dot in the Gulf between Venezuela and Trinidad: freedom. The officers don't take we on much; they don't lock up too tight, because where it have to run? We can't go nowhere. Or so they feel.

Straight from the cell, me and Richards, my cellmate, we stroll out.

Officer Babylon watching TV. We tell him exactly where we going: "Down by the water, Boss. To light up, li'l bit."

"Allyuh going and smoke? Or allyuh going and bull?" he say, squawking like a seagull.

"Nah, we could do that anytime we want in the cell," I say, not because me and Richards in any bullerman thing, but because that kinda fleck-up answer is the best way to block Babylon from saying something worse, something that might

---

1. Commonly shortened by locals to "the Bocas", this is the collective geographic name for the several small straits between the northwestern point of Trinidad and the Venezuelan coast. However, on most maps it is not translated as plural, but rather as the singular, "The Dragon's Mouth".

make me lose my head and buss he throat.

Tonight is not to fight. No, when your head in the dragon mouth, you ease it out real slow.

Me and Richards trot down the incline, to the nibbling edge of the water. The place warm, warm—not a breeze blowing, but that good for us because the water go be flat. It have a full moon, though, grinning like it know what we planning and so it come out for spite, to make sure everybody see we. We didn't expect this damn moon—I shoulda check beforehand, my mistake— but is do or die tonight. All the dominoes done line up and people waiting on we.

So, me and Richards stand up, watching the silver water and sighing, like if we's really lovers. Me ain't know what he thinking, but I studying Consuela, she there on the other side, on the mainland. Not Venezuela (although that's where she come from), I mean the big island, Trinidad. Consuela working in one of them so-called "guesthouse" in Pleasantview. She know I coming, at least I think so—I did send message with my pardnah, Stench: "Pack and get ready. I comin' for you Thursday night."

Consuela waiting; she can't wait forever—she done wait too long already. Time to move.

"Light the thing, nah, bai," I tell Richards, "before the man get suspish."

Richards pull a li'l spliff and a lighter from he pants pocket. He take a pull, I take two, we blow out the smoke and the air start to smell like herb.

I rest down the joint on a rock, and prop it up nice, nice. "You ready?"

"Yeah, let we go."

With that, me and Richards walk into the sea and just keep walking till we disappear. We lucky: not everybody could do what we doing. Only a few fellas on this prison island, even counting officers, could swim good. But Richards say he born and grow down Ste. Madeleine near a pond, he say nobody in the village was faster than he. But I tell him fresh water different to salt, and pond have edge; the sea ain't got none. But he say that don't matter. Me, I born in this Gulf: Icacos, to be exact. If Trinidad is a boots, Icacos is the toe. On a clear, clear day, we used to see Venezuela plain as we hand. My father is a fisherman, he father was a fisherman, and so it go and so it go . . . all the way back through history. From small, I was always on the pirogue with Daddy; I learn to swim before I could walk, I learn to dive before I could read and write. That's why I slapping this water, making it splatter outta my way, like is nothing more than melt-down ghee.

Left, right, left, right.

I did tell Stench to wait by the next small island, a li'l cove it have there. Wait and keep the boat quiet, no engine till I reach. Bring change of clothes, I did say. And have a car waiting in Carenage. We heading straight for Pleasantview, straight for Consuela. By that time, they go sound the alarm on the prison island, and while they huntin' for we in the north-west, we go dash down South, to Icacos. I have to see Daddy and Mammy before I leave for Venezuela. I have to collect back the money Daddy holding for me. With that, me and Consuela go set up weself nice, nice, nice, back in Tucupita, she hometown.

Left, right, left, right. That cove is half a kilometer from here—so the map say. Left, right, left, right. Half a kilometer is about 1,600 feet. That's all. Feet. Freedom is just feet away from me. And freedom have a next name: Consuela. Consuela, Consuela. A kind of madness take over: I turn barracuda in the water, one arm over the next, I going faster and faster. I ain't feeling nothing, I ain't 'fraid nothing, I not looking back, I not going back.

I hear a siren and I know is for we.

I shout for Richards and he shout back but he sounding far, like he lagging behind.

"Richards!" I bawl again, "they comin! Swim!"

That's all I could say because I pushing through the water, pushing hard. *I not going back!*

Then I hear a vessel, the Coast Guard fastboat. Then voices, Richards bawling, other voices. It sound like he fighting with them; he not going easy. I sorry for him but I glad same time, because them so busy with he, I get chance to swim faster, push harder, lungs burnin' till I feel I go dead.

"Jesus!" I gasp and spit brine.

Jesus used to lime with fisherman, so he go hear me. I only have energy to swing my hand one last time and I touch a log. I latch on . . . and name it Hallelujah. Hallelujah keep my head above water till I reach the cove. I can't believe I actually reach, I 'fraid to let go Hallelujah, but them fellas grab and pull me on the pirogue.

We take off for Carenage.

I so tired, I barely breathing, but I have to ask Stench, "You tell she I comin'?"

He say, "Yes, bai. And I just talk to she. She ready and waiting."

She glances again at the clock, strategically placed on the side wall of her room. From any angle, she is always able check if a customer's time is up. A self-taught trick—that, and many more. It is just after 10:00 p.m. Sunil sent a message earlier to say, "He coming tonight; pack and get ready." So yes, she's packing, but with only half a heart. She is not at all sure if she should believe in him.

Sunil has been in jail for the last year.

In Venezuela, jails are never easy to walk out of, but this is Trinidad—everything is different, easier in many ways. The night-news talks of prisoners and their "rights". She isn't sure what exactly that means, though, and if she has those too.

Consuela shrugs like she's taking off an invisible blouse, but her doubts remain, even as she moves the last two items from her clothes drawer. She dumps them into the faded nylon duffel bag Sunil gave her seventeen and a half months ago—she's been counting. She's collected lots more clothes, nicer clothes since then: tights, frothy blouses, jeans and pretty lacy panties, all bought in Pleasantview Junction from roadside people who shout, "Mamacita, take a walk inside! Take a walk inside!" They are accustomed to seeing "Vennies" scurrying around the back streets—to them, every Latina is a Venezuelan whore—so they take her money and ask no questions. She pays a higher price for their silence. She is safe in Pleasantview. As long as her Boss Lady makes sure policemen have free service at the guesthouse, she is safe. She has never even thought of boarding a maxitaxi and going anywhere else in Trinidad. Where can she run without a passport and a man to protect her from other men? Here, at least, she has Mr. Jagroop.

She approaches the closet where her "good clothes" hang—a couple dresses and some shinier, more bling-bling versions of the same things that were in the drawer, most acquired only recently. The $200 Sunil has been sending now and then can't do much for her, but she struck jackpot a few months ago when Mr. Jagroop approached Boss Lady about "permanent arrangements". Friday nights with Consuela became his, and he pays dearly for them. But he can afford, Boss Lady says, because he's a businessman and, rumor has it, he'll be a candidate for the next local elections. He is a good man to fuck.

Consuela backs away from the closet and sits on the edge of her bed, staring at the gold lycra of a jumpsuit. She is worth something here in Pleasantview. Does she really want to leave? She isn't even sure she's the same person who fell in love with Sunil, who promised him, "I will wait," last year, when he'd called her to say he was turning himself in to police. But she is very sure she's no longer the tender seventeen-year-old who did as her mother asked and got on a boat with Sunil and his father and the other men, to cross the Gulf. No, this *eighteen*-year-old Consuela has trained herself to let go of many things, to squelch and drown other things. She's learned how to focus only on the words spoken during those last moments with her Mama. She has trained herself not to remember her own dread and her own secret trembling at being married off to a boy she barely knew, to a land she'd never seen.

"Promise me, she . . . only one," Mama pleaded with Sunil's father before he left Tucupita. He always visited Mama's bed whenever he docked in the village; he always paid with cash but tipped with foodstuff. He was one of the honest smugglers; his promise carried weight with her.

"Yes, only she," Sunil's father said. "I don't bring in people on my boat. I only making exception this time because of my son. He over-want she."

"And he will married, *sí?*"

"Yes, we's Hindu. Is no problem to married—she seventeen, he nineteen—they old enough. By next year, my house full up with pretty, pretty, fair skin baby and thing."

"She will work, teach *en la escuela,* okay? *Ella habla inglés perfectamente.*"

Sunil's father silenced Mama with a hug. "I promise you, she go have a good, easy life. Plenty better than out here," he said, pointing his chin at their home: a concrete slab surrounded by roofing sheets.

He turned to leave then, but Mama followed, explaining her fears. "*Mi otra hija,* Marisol, she take boat from Güiria last year. Too full. News say everybody die. I *no lo creo, pero* we hear nothing . . . *nada más.* I still . . . *Yo no creo, no lo creo.*" Then Mama grabbed his elbow, as if he hadn't paid his bill for last night. "You help Consuela find she sister, *mi* Marisol?" she asked.

"Look," Sunil's father said, peeling her off, "Trinidad is a big place. All I could tell you: Consuela safe with we."

And she was safe, at first. The boat slipped as easily onto the sands of Icacos as she slipped into the household of Sunil and his family. They smiled at her but cooked things she didn't know how to eat: no *cachapas con queso,* only roti and choka; no *pabellón,* only dhal and rice and curry. Everything was strange, and she understood little when they spoke to each other—too fast, and not the English she knew from school—and Sunil's mother made her clean and wash for most of each day. But Sunil spoke to her slowly when they were alone. He cooed like she was a baby. It was from him she learned that the pundit was coming at the end of the week to marry them. Sunil said he wanted to wait until afterward, to have sex as man and wife. He was Hindu, yes, but he went to the Presbyterian Church sometimes with his mother, so he knew better than to sin.

But, before the wedding could take place, Sunil's father came running in one day, and ordered her to pack. All the plastic bags she'd brought from Venezuela were scattered about; she didn't even know what they'd done with her little rolling suitcase.

"Now! Now!" he said to Sunil. "Get she ready. Police coming."

Sunil threw her stuff into his own duffel bag. Then he and his father bundled her into their van and drove to a Chinese man in a nearby village. Sunil's father asked for two thousand. "No. Fit-teen handrey," the man countered. Sunil's father said, "Sold," and collected, in a back room behind the Chinese restaurant, his fifteen hundred greasy American dollars.

The memory makes Consuela pitch herself backward onto the bed. She plucks, from between the pillows, her virgin white teddy bear—a Valentine's gift from Mr. Jagroop. With both hands, she holds it above her and stares into its dead-fish eyes. She wonders, for the millionth time, if any police had been coming at all, that day in Icacos. Or had Sunil's father made up the whole story? Had he been planning to sell her all along but couldn't bear to tell Sunil? Or had Sunil known? Back then, she believed Sunil was innocent. And she'd even believed when he tearfully said he was "coming back soon" to redeem her from the Chinese man.

But he hadn't come back. The *chino* locked her in a room with a Colombiana, and every few days or so, they were tied and raped side by side ("Yes, fellas," *chino* would say, "break them in good.") And yes, they had broken her insides with their *machetes*, chopped her up real good inside, severed whichever artery carried feeling and pain and faith and hope and love. And when she and the Colombiana weren't being raped, they would pray and tell each other, *"Hermana, tienes que ser fuerte, piense en tu familia allá."* For five weeks they repeated that. Out loud and in their heads too, under the black and brown bodies of these strange men who dripped cologne-water but smelled of fish, rancid coconut oil and engine grease. Consuela proved the more popular of the two, and one day *chino* came in wagging his finger and said, "Like how you more white-looking than she, and your hair more yellow, you go be a big, big hit and make good money up north."

Consuela was transferred to his sister, Boss Lady, in Pleasantview. To this pussy-pink house on Panco Lane. Still small-bodied, still seventeen, but she'd hardened to forty inside—yet Boss Lady told the customers, "Consuela is fifteen."

Sunil came one day. He spent a long time talking with her, cursing as he told her how *chino* had refused to let him see her, and then crying as she told him what *chin*o had made her do. Then, he spent a long time talking with Boss Lady. Afterwards, he looked happy. His face beaming and his shoulders high when he said, "She say I could buy you back. Just hold on, babes, I coming for you."

That was a fifteen months ago, and still, she must say she's fifteen. Customers still call her "whitey" and "blondie", but what she sees of herself in the closet mirror as she works is *negra como el carbón*. Sure, Boss Lady pays her well, lets her send cash back home using the Chinese money-line, lets her have a cellphone so she can lie to Mama every week about how the money is made *("Sí, Mama, soy profesora de inglés"),* lets her shop in the Junction, lets her have everything—except her passport and freedom.

But Consuela never complains, because she isn't sure what she would do differently, anyway, if she had those things. Mama sent her here to earn money and find Marisol—it was never in the plan that she should seek a life and dreams and happiness of her own. She is careful not to reach too high, *donde sus manos no pueden alcanzar.*

She rolls onto her side, draws teddy into her bosom and curls up on the bed, her place of work. She makes a hurried Sign of the Cross . . . *en el nombre del Padre, del Hijo* . . . but it doesn't make her feel any more blessed or protected or any less alone. She remains dried out and brittle inside. She is terrified to risk even a tiny spark of belief.

By the time we reach the jetty in Carenage, I catch back my breath and my senses and all the li'l pieces of myself that the sea was threatening to drown. We move through the night like some cat looking for fish and I stand up in the darkest dark, under a hog plum tree, to change my clothes. I put on the dry ones Stench bring.

"Come, let we move," I say, talking like the boss of the operation again—I ain't hear myself sound so in a whole year.

Stench bump fist with the two other fellas—I don't know them, them don't know me, and it better so—they jump in a next car and drive off. Them head west, we head east to Pleasantview.

Stench secondhand Toyota patchy with flashband and moving slow, but my blood fuel-injected. I hype up, I nervous, I happy, I could lift up this damn car and run with it—you would swear I sniff coke or something. Daddy did bring in some blocks one time, and I did watch the customer dip-in a finger, taste the powder, then bawl, "Shiiit! That's the damn thing self. Pure, pure. Thing to blow man brain out they head."

"Thanks, eh," I tell Stench, clapping him on the back over and over, like he choking and need help. "You's a damn good friend. You been a brother to me," I keep saying. Is true: Stench was there with me, on Daddy boat, when we did bring across Consuela. And is he-self used to go with me, by Lee Loy Restaurant every week to look for she. And then, when the Chinee Mafia send she north, to Pleasantview, is Stench used to drive me up the road every week, in this same old Toyota, to check on she. He do me plenty favors, but he know, just like I know: he owing me more than I owing he. Is *me* did take the rap with the police, I never turn informer, I never call he name. I did make one single request from him before I walk myself in the police station: "Every month, go by Daddy, he go give you a li'l change; take it for Consuela."

"How she looking?" I ask Stench—I does ask that every time he visit me in prison.

"Good, good," he say. "She taking care of sheself."

He does always say that, and it does always make me feel good to hear it. I did promise to handle she, as a man does handle he woman. The five hundred I sending every month, through Stench, it ain't much but it making a point: no matter who she fuck, she still my woman. Any man could climb on top of she, but I's the onliest man making jail for she.

Watch, nah: when Boss Lady did say I coulda buy Consuela and she passport back for fifty thousand, I nearly fall down and kiss she old, stinking toe—fuss I was glad—it had a hope for we. I went straight home and tell Daddy that I done with that petty smuggling life on the boat. He did cuss me and call me neemakharam, but I didn't care. I went and get a good contract-work with the oil company—driving truck and boat, digging hole, fixing engine, anything they tell me do—and I did start to save, save, save. But the funds wasn't piling up fast enough, and Consuela keep crying every time I went to see she, so I had was to think fast. I team up with Stench and some other fellas to make a li'l lagniappe on the side. But the oil company catch on and tell police "industrial tools worth more than US$10,000 have gone missing." I did give Daddy my cut to hold, and I plead guilty, thinking My Honor woulda give me a small jail, but the fucker hit me with seven years—big jail, on the prison island, far far far from Consuela.

I did cry like a snatty-nose baby in the courtroom.

"So, bai, let we go through the plan one last time," I tell Stench. "Everything hadda move like clockwork tonight."

He say after we get Consuela we heading down Icacos to collect my money and all the groceries my father done stockpile—garlic, baby milk, pampers, toilet paper, tin juice—things that scarce in Venezuela. Then, Stench go take we out in the pirogue to a condemn oil platform in the Gulf. Then, a man Daddy does do business with go pick we up and take we the rest of the way, upriver, to Tucupita. Consuela go be home with she mother and nephew-them again. And we go have enough to set up a nice li'l shop and have a quiet life.

I like the plan. No, I love it. I stick my head out the car window and search till I find the moon. It there behind me, like I leave it hanging up over the prison island. What they doing now with Richards, I wonder. I sorry for the man, but better he than me, oui. I know they looking for me, I know they coming, but all I need to do is keep moving and stay ahead of this blasted, deceitful moon.

The moment Consuela dozes off, Marisol's face floats up. Not the Marisol she'd always been—red-painted lips, black-lined eyes, blonde hair wild—but the Marisol she'd stripped down to, the last time Consuela saw her, twenty-four months ago, back in Venezuela. She'd worn no makeup and her hair was pulled back and braided into one long, golden rope—if only it could have saved her! She wore a simple T-shirt, jeans, sneakers. She wanted to enter her new life, she said, on the other side of the Gulf, looking respectable. She'd believed and trusted the man from the Christian group when he said they would resettle her in Trinidad.

Consuela sees it all again in her dream, how she pleaded with her older sister, *"Hermana, no! No le creas,"* but Marisol wouldn't listen. Manuelito—only five years old—was dead, the hospital in their village had run out of medicine for the infection he'd gotten from a broken beer bottle. *"Me quedan dos hijos,"* Marisol said to Consuela, *"los voy a salvar."* Then she walked off with Manuelito's old superhero backpack—*Los Increíbles*—and disappeared. Consuela has asked and asked, but nobody in Trinidad has ever heard of Marisol Romero Silva . . . *de Tucupita.*

Consuela startles from her sleep. She looks at the clock; it has only been a ten-minute doze but the night has deepened, it seems. She opens the casement windows wide, craving fresh cool air, but no breeze blows her way; craving the lick of sea spray on her cheek, but she is too far from the Gulf. She walks to the door, wishing there was someone she could talk to about Sunil and his offer of freedom, but she cannot trust the other girls; they are all locals.

In the middle of the room she stands, like one of the many little *islas*, emerald shards scattered in the Bocas waters between Trinidad and Venezuela. Not one of them, no matter how hard they yearn, can reattach what time and tide has carved off—it would be a useless effort: *aquí estoy, aquí me quedo.*

She calls Mr. Jagroop, who always speaks kindly to her and is always gentle—almost apologetic and fatherly—after he's finished with her. He answers right away. She tells him Sunil is coming and she's not sure what to do. She hopes Jagroop will beg her to stay, offer her something more than a life in Icacos baking roti on a tawa, pretending to be normal, pretending to feel things she can no longer feel.

"You talk to the man?" Jagroop asks.

"No."

"So how you know he really coming tonight?" She hears submerged laughter in the ripples of Jagroop's voice.

"His friend . . . he call me, he say—"

"Girl, don't worry your head," Jagroop cuts her off. "I don't think he coming, nah. But, if he show up, don't answer, don't come out your room. Just call me. I go handle it."

"Okay, okay, yes. I sleep now," she says, eager to get off the phone. He has made her feel childish and naive, when she's been trying oh so hard to be the opposite. She decides that whatever happens, she will not call Mr. Jagroop back. She will handle this on her own.

"Wait," he says, before she hangs up. "I real like how you comport yuhself tonight. You didn't have to tell me nuttin'. It show you have more class than that guesthouse. You's a real nice girl, and I been thinking 'bout something lately, and now you help me make up my mind. Tomorrow, when I come across, I going and have a chat with Boss Lady: is high time I take you outta there. You deserve better than that, babes."

"Oh, yes, yes, Mr. Jagroop," Consuela says, her heart thumping. "*Gracias*, Mr. Jagroop."

She switches the phone off so Sunil and his friend cannot reach her, so they will get tired of calling and just drive off—*if* they do show up tonight.

She tries, in vain, to accept her own decision and to rest. Sleep is like something she's lost under the bed and can't find no matter how much she twists and turns or how hard she squints. After a while, she lies flat on her back, staring at the pink, cotton-candy knot of mosquito netting. She kicks it, begins counting its swings but ends up counting how much more she'll be able to send to her mother, *if* Mr. Jagroop sets her up as his mistress. It would make sense of everything: her journey and the death of who she was before Icacos, Marisol's journey and death in the Gulf, Manuelito's gangrene, the worries of Mama raising Marisol's two other boys.

But Mr. Jagroop might change his mind—it's his right.

He might change tomorrow and never ask Boss Lady, or he might change after a week . . . two weeks . . . a month: take her, then get bored or get mad and bring her back.

Milagros, Señor! Consuela prays. Hadn't she witnessed a miracle happen last year, for Luz, the Dominicana who used to be in the back bedroom: a businessman from Port of Spain bought her, *como un perrito en la ventana,* set her up in a cute apartment—she'd come back to visit and shown pictures. Luz had even given Consuela her old, dog-eared New Testament, because she didn't need it anymore. She'd bought a whole Bible now, she'd said, a big fancy one with gold on the edges.

Consuela flicks on the bedside lamp and stares at the half-empty duffel on the floor. The half-Bible is in there. She kneels and feels around in the bag until she finds the book she hasn't opened in months. A blue rectangle no bigger than her palm. *Nuevo Testamento,* its cover declares; below those words a little golden diamond, then *Salmos y Proverbios,* and below those words a golden jar in a golden circle, then: *Este Libro No Sera Vendido.* Consuela's soul flinches at the reminder: some things should not be for sale. She flips the pages with her thumb, wondering what to read. What chapter, what verse? What wisdom did the Lord leave behind *para una putita perdida?* She sandwiches the book, page edges facing her, and digs both thumbs into its flesh as if peeling a tangerine. The book opens and her eyes fall on 1 *Corintios* 13:13:

> *Y ahora permanecen la fe, la esperanza y el amor, estos tres;*
> *pero el mayor de ellos es el amor.*

Consuela spreads the book wide on the bed, reads the verse again and again to teddy, then clutches the page against her chest as if staunching a mortal wound. She doesn't have much *faith* left in Sunil, she barely has any *hope* at all, in anything. But it's possible she does have *love*—Sunil's love. *If* he's broken out of jail to come get her, *if* he actually shows up, that will be the sign she needs. It doesn't matter that she's still angry at him, or that she doesn't know if she could love him or anyone anymore. If *he* loves *her*, she will go with him. She will follow this half-Bible—it worked for Luz, she reminds herself—she will not flip and flop *como una merluza* gasping on the floor of a fishing boat.

When we pull up outside, the place dark, dark like everybody sleeping.

"Bai, me eh know ho-house does close on a Thursday night?" Stench say, killing the engine.

"Me neither," I say. "But this one different to them places we know. This place is for big-shot fellas and thing."

Stench start to mumble 'bout how he money and he prick as good as any man, but I shush him. "Call she, nah?" I say.

The phone ring off while I sitting down here jiggling my leg like it catch malaria. She not answering. He call again but same thing.

"You want me blow the horn?" he say.

"Don't be a ass," I say, as I crack open the car door.

With his black skin and red jersey, he look like a vex coral-snake when he hiss, "Watch yourself. Somebody go see you and call police."

I walk to the gate, then back to the fence—half wall, half chain link with a hedge poking through. I studying the house. If I remember correct, Consuela room is the front one, right there. But suppose they move she to a next one? A year is a long fuckin' time.

The dark curtain in the front room get split by a shank of orangish light, like from a low-watt bulb or a lamp. Some fellas mighta take it as a sign, a caution light, but my brain take it as: on your marks, get set . . . and then I gone. Close my eyes, brace one foot on the wall and fling myself against the chain link fence, as if I flinging a net off a boat. The bougainvillea have fingernail and teeth; it grabbing and pulling and ripping into me. I fighting it, not knowing if I going over or through, and then suddenly I land on the other side, in the grass, skin burning like I get rub down with Congo pepper.

A voice say, "Su-neel," and when I look up, Consuela in the same front window, watching down on me with she hand over she mouth like she shock.

"Baby," I say, the word come through my nose like a breath. I start to run before I even stand up good, so I moving across the grass like a zandolee on all fours, catching the ground then raising my body, becoming a man again by the time I reach the window.

"Shhh," she say.

I lift up my two hand as if I back in church with my mother, praising the Lord, and I say, "Jump. I go catch you. Is only a small drop. Don't frighten." But I trembling, my whole body hot and shaking like a outboard engine. Suppose she say no? Suppose she don't love me again? Suppose she have a new big-shot man? But when she throw she leg over the sill, I get my answer. Then she say, "Wait," and pull back, making my heart sputter, until she reappear and throw down a bag—the same duffel I did give she so long ago. I catch it, then I catch she, overbalance and we fall in the grass, roll and separate like one big, ripe breadfruit that fall and buss in two.

Consuela climbs Sunil's body like a ladder, then eases herself down the other side, hops onto the pavement. He follows, lands in a squat then springs up and claims her in a bear hug. He smells as he always did, as the rapists in Icacos did, of the Gulf—saltwater, fuel and fish. Her arms flop and she pulls away in a panic. She cannot go through with this: she cannot live with Sunil's father who sold her, Sunil's mother who worked her like a slave. This freedom is not free, and she is a pauper who cannot repay Sunil's love. Her body twitches with readiness to run to the gate, to shake, shake, shake till they let her back in. Then she looks up at Sunil and, in a streetlamp's ray, sees his eyes, watery, red and pleading. No other man has ever looked at her in this naked way. Some delicate strand of emotion moves, brushing against her heart then floating away, only to return and entwine itself when he says, "Girl, I so sorry. Come, nah? I taking you back home, we going and stay, back by your mother-them."

Her breath catches at this news. *Dios mío!* Sunil is offering to leave his country and his family for hers, to become an exile for her, to exchange places. This is the sign the Bible predicted, this is *amor . . . el mayor de todos*.

When Sunil opens the back door, she scrambles into the car. He passes her the faded bag and she hugs it, in place of the teddy bear left behind on the bed.

"You alright there?" he asks, and when she says yes, he gets into the front passenger seat and orders Stench to "bun road." Consuela hugs the bag tighter, closes her eyes and says a silent thank you: *Gracias a Dios por este milagro. Gracias a Dios.*

They haven't moved far, though, when she feels the car roll and heave like a boat.

She opens her eyes to the glaring headlights of a Jeep parked on their side of the narrow lane. She ducks into the shade of Sunil's headrest just as he and Stench curse, *What the mudda*—and raise their arms against the light. Then, the Jeep swings across the road, blocking their escape.

The Jeep's front doors open and a male voice shouts, "Police! Police!"

"Sunil," Consuela bleats, but he's busy telling Stench, "Reverse, reverse!"

"You mad or what? They go kill we, bai," Stench screeches.

"I not going back. Reverse," Sunil insists, grabbing the gearstick. The two friends fight, but two firecracker sounds make them freeze.

The voice from beyond orders, "Put your two hand outside the glass!"

The boys comply, Sunil crying now, moaning, "Oh God, Oh God . . ."

The same booming voice says, "Open the door from outside and lie down on the ground! Face down! Now!"

Consuela remains bolt upright in the back seat; sweat glues her to the upholstery. Afraid to move, she whimpers a litany of Spanish words, gibberish even to her, as she watches the boys surrender. This is a movie, she is watching a movie, or this is a bad dream . . . yes, she has had many bad dreams since coming to Trinidad but she always wakes up warm and safe in her whore-house bed. But this dream gets even more scary when Corporal Sharpe, a regular at the guesthouse, steps out from behind the Jeep's door. He is wearing a bulletproof vest and walking sideways like a giant crab, his gun aimed at Sunil, who is flat on the pavement. The other policeman approaches Stench in the same way.

But what will they do to her? Consuela wails as she glimpses her future: Boss Lady can't save her now! They will rape her in the police station, they will rape her in the jail, they will swallow her whole in the detention center where they send all *Venezolanas*, and then they will shit her back out in Tucupita, back with her Mama, back with nothing.

What was it all for? *Fue todo en vano?*

As if by some spell of *brujeria*, her door opens, someone reaches in and drags her out, drags her along the pavement, back in the direction of the guesthouse, until she is next to a big black vehicle. Blinded by tears, she doesn't recognize *el demonio* until he speaks, "You bitch! You dutty li'l bitch, you! Playing games with me, eh? I go teach you a lesson here tonight."

Jagroop. He cuffs her face and she falls, her ears ringing with the sound her radio makes when signals fail across the

Bocas. Jagroop kicks her, over and over, while she becomes an eel on the gritty pavement. Somewhere behind the shrill noise, Sunil's voice sputters, "Leave she alone! Leave she! I go kill yuh!" and her body vibrates with the frantic drumming of feet.

"Stop, boy, stop!" Corporal Sharpe screams.

Consuela opens her eyes and foresees what is about to happen. She opens wide her lungs, her heart, her throat, her mouth to warn Sunil, "No! Don't come!" but her English deserts her and she hears her own stranded cry, "No vengas!" at the exact moment Jagroop's boot lands on her ribs and there is a loud pop.

Her eyes meet Sunil's across the cold concrete. He bleeds, and she bleeds too, but she is the one who wishes to die.

Endangered Species

OMAR SAT, UNCOMFORTABLE, IN THE FRONT seat of the maxi-taxi minivan. His lanky frame was hunched and contorted, his face puffed-up like a country crapaud. He was pissed. He'd been pissed when he left his mother's house in the quiet, turtle-watching village of Matura about an hour ago, and he was pissed now as the maxi neared the bustling hub of Pleasantview Junction. He didn't want to be back in Pleasantview—but his mother, Josephine, wouldn't listen. He didn't want to return to the tiny, suffocating room with the chicken-wire window where he rented from the Jagroops. He didn't want to spend another day of his life bagging groceries at the Save-U Supermarket. And to make matters worse, he didn't want the old, fragile picture-frame in his duffel bag—but, this morning, Josephine had made him take it anyway.

The usual buildings, trees and savannahs whooshed past. Omar sat tense, wincing with every pothole, gripping the duffel's strap, bracing the bag with his knee to keep it from falling. Josephine would never forgive him if he broke the stupid picture: him and his father on the beach with a leatherback turtle. The photo had long ago faded and become welded to the glass, time and heat making them one.

One 8 x 10 booby-trap.

Its only purpose was to ensnare Omar in dangerous thoughts of what was missing in his life—what *had been* missing—for the past eleven years. Jacob van der Zee: high-and-mighty turtle scientist, dashing Dutchman, runaway father. He'd abandoned Omar and Josephine when Omar was six, leaving the boy confused as to whether the paralyzing feeling he got, every time he looked at the picture, was raw hatred or, merely, sour love.

Screech! About two miles from Pleasantview Junction, the maxi suddenly swerved. Came to a lurching stop. A grating, straining noise followed as the driver retried the engine. There was . . . nothing. He twisted around to face the passengers and barked, "Allyuh come out, come out. We shut down."

A collective steups went up—everyone, including Omar, sucking their teeth. The twelve passengers in the back of the maxi began turtling out. Omar took a moment to slow his heart-beat and rotate the shoulder yanked by the bag, then he hopped from the front seat.

On the pavement, the passengers had encircled the driver, demanding a refund. As Omar eased his bag out, he noticed a short, black Rasta-man watching him cut-eye.

"What you say, Big-Red? Ain't the man should give we back we money?"

Omar couldn't believe his bad luck. Just because of his six-foot-four height, just because he looked big and strong, people always tried to recruit him for their dirty work. But why today? Today, when he was so anxious to get to his room. Today, when the sole challenge of his journey was to keep the picture frame unbroken. He wanted no run-ins with these Pleasantview people. He didn't know how to cuss like them and he'd never learned how to fight. So, like a basketballer, he swiveled out of the jittery mob. He crossed the road and began speed-walking toward the Junction. Behind him, the Rasta called out, "Like you's a li'l mama-man, or what!" But Omar had heard that one before in high school, along with "Lonesome Dove," "Big Pussy," and countless other names only the quiet boys got called.

Two miles. With this heavy bag, in this nine o'clock sun. Omar trudged forward, wondering if the maxi shutting down was some kind of supernatural punishment. For the fights he'd had with Josephine this weekend; for the way he'd stormed out this morning: slamming the door extra hard, so her beloved crucifix rattled and fell to the floor.

His nostrils picked up the rankness of the rubbish-filled drain alongside the pavement. And his ears registered a rising chaos: horns, engines, exhausts; they clashed with voices, sirens, reggae. Every time Omar set foot in Pleasantview he felt overwhelmed. It was so hard to tell music from noise, the good places from the bad places, the good guys from the bad guys. Take that Rasta, for instance: he could've been joking, but he could've just as well been picking a fight.

Omar squinted as, up ahead at the corner of Evans Street, his landlord, Mr. Jagroop's fruit and vegetable stand, The Horn of Plenty, came into sight. Sunlight shimmered on its white, oil-paint walls in a way that reminded Omar of inside a conch-shell. Mr. Jagroop was another Pleasantview person Omar found confusing. He cussed out his wife every single day, called her "cunt" and "bitch" like it was her first name, and yet the man was the best father to his lazy, rum-guzzling son, Manohar. A couple months ago, when Omar had just moved in, he'd noticed Mr. Jagroop loading up the produce truck every day with no help. One morning, Omar had summoned the courage to offer; but Mr. Jagroop had grunted, "Nah. It should be Mannie helping. That boy over-lazy! Is that old bitch have him so. But what I go do? Is my son."

Since then, Omar had become almost obsessed with Mr. Jagroop. He waited every morning to hear the old man cussing, then his rubber slippers on the stairs; then Omar spied on him. First, puja, Hindu prayers by a little shrine in the yard. Then Mr. Jagroop washed and loaded both trucks: his as well as his son's; then he and Mannie left for work together. He was, to Omar's eyes, exactly what a father should be. Omar wished he could know the old man better, study him up close like a rare species, solve the mystery of how one man could have such different sides. Josephine had said, "You is the newcomer, Omar. *You* have to try again with your landlord-and-them." But Omar couldn't think of how to make another approach to Mr. Jagroop.

He came alongside The Horn of Plenty and peered in.

The place seemed deserted except for disgusting Mannie, who sat at the cash register chewing his nails and spitting them into a crate of grapefruit. Then the hammock at the back of the shed moved. Omar glimpsed Mr. Jagroop. He swung gently, stroking his pumpkin belly and humming the mournful Indian music of a nearby radio. In his hand, he contemplated a mango.

"Morning," Omar bleated with a timid wave.

Father and son startled. Mannie merely grunted while Mr.

Jagroop called out, "Morning, Omar. Where you toting that big bag this hour?"

"Home, Mr. Jagroop. But the maxi shut-down. I hustling to the Junction to get a car."

The old man shot from the hammock like a stone from a sling. He shoved the mango into one pocket of his khaki shorts and pulled a bunch of keys from the other. With a big grin, he walked toward Omar saying, "Come, come, I go give you a drop."

Grateful, Omar folded his length into the truck's tiny cab and balanced the duffel on his knees. Mr. Jagroop raised a bushy eyebrow and said, "Humph! Is gold inside there, or what? Put that beast in the tray, nah."

"No, is just—"

Before Omar could say, "something that could break", Mr. Jagroop cut in. "So, you busy, son? Or you have time? I have a few stops to make first." Pulling away from the curb, he added, "Plus, I feel you is the man to help me with something. You don't mind?"

A *few* stops? Omar wanted to get to his room as quickly as possible. To unload the picture, get it off his conscience and stow it away somewhere safe, where he'd never have to look at it. But Mr. Jagroop had asked *him* a favor, made it clear that Omar was *the man* to help. Omar wasn't sure what was involved but he knew he couldn't say no. He'd been wanting an inroad like this for too long.

Their first stop was quick: the bank, in the same shopping plaza as the Save-U where Omar worked. While he waited in the truck, he thought of how Josephine had reacted yesterday when he'd said he would stay in Matura, find a job there, where he felt comfortable and understood life, where he had a few friends. To hell with Pleasantview, he'd told Josephine. Packing groceries like a maniac—but never fast enough for the Save-U Manager—twelve hours a day, Monday to Saturday. It made Omar feel he was on a five-day deadline, like a pregnant turtle. Flap, flap, flap, work, work, work—but, in his case, for what? To deliver his dirty laundry and crisp salary to Josephine every Sunday. Then, every Monday, to slouch back to Pleasantview and begin the cycle all over again. Seventeen years old and wasting life, Omar had complained.

Josephine had straightened slowly, swiped the suds straight down from her elbows, back into the washtub, before turning to Omar. "You mad or what? It ain't have nowhere in Matura that paying what you making in Pleasantview."

Sitting there in Mr. Jagroop's truck, Omar still believed she was wrong. He could easily be a tour guide at some eco-resort. Nobody knew Matura beach like him; nobody knew turtles like him. Jacob had shared so much during their walks; Omar had never forgotten any of it—not even the sound of Jacob's voice. And so many midnights, when Josephine was snoring in her bed, Omar had snuck out to the beach to learn more, to watch the mother-turtles in nesting season.

There, Omar's argument snagged.

Nesting season. Tour guides in Matura only had work in nesting season.

He glanced across at Save-U where he worked now, and would always have work, every day, all year round—even public holidays,

Yes, but he still had no friends. Yesterday, Josephine had scolded him, "Listen, Matura can't do one ass for you. So you better start treating Pleasantview like is your future. Put your whole self in it, son. Try again with them people."

Just then, Mr. Jagroop's grinning face reappeared in the driver's-side window. He held two sno-cones—and offered one to Omar. A perfect globe of crushed ice, soaked with red syrup and wearing a white pope-hat of condensed milk. It looked cooling and delicious, so Omar stretched to accept, noticing, as Mr. Jagroop climbed into the truck, an unsealed envelope, thick with money, jutting from the old man's pocket.

They swung out of the parking lot and back onto the main road. Between bites of ice, Mr. Jagroop chatted as if they took road-trips together all the time, and Omar began to feel school-boyish again.

"So you hear the news?" Mr. Jagroop said. "Your landlord might be a Member-a-Parliament soon, son. They ask me to be the UNC candidate."

"But that real good, Mr. Jagroop!"

"Yeah, only the background checks now. They does real dig-up in your past, you know? By the time they finish, they know everything about a man—down to what size jockey-shorts he does wear."

"True?"

"That's why I have a li'l favor to ask. A errand. I can't send Mannie. But I need somebody I could trust as much. I was there in the hammock thinking, 'Lord, who?' and then *bam!* You walk up. You is the quietest fella I ever see. I know I could trust you."

In his head, Omar repeated Mr. Jagroop's words, "...somebody

I could trust as much. . . ." As much as Mannie? Or as much as a son? There was a difference. Omar wouldn't want to be equated with Mannie—lazy and always reeking of rum. But, for Mr. Jagroop to trust Omar like a son—well, *that* Omar didn't mind. He answered, "For sure, Mr. Jagroop. But what it is?"

Jagroop patted his pocket. "I just need you to run inside and hand somebody this. You think you could manage?"

Omar was still nodding as they turned onto clogged Evans Street. On one side, the University campus sprawled, bounded by their neighborhood of East Pleasantview.

"So Omar, is which village you from again? Matura, ain't?" Mr. Jagroop asked, gearing the truck down to a crawl.

Omar nodded distractedly, "Mmm-hmm," taking advantage of the traffic to macco inside the University fence. Boys and girls, no older than him probably, reclining on the lawn. Some read fat books. Others chatted. Under a samaan tree, a couple kissed. If he'd had a real father, maybe Omar might've been among them, studying something—anything—related to the sea; and maybe he would've had a girlfriend too, somebody pretty—but quiet like him.

"All them north coast villages is the same. Turtles, turtles, turtles. Not so?"

"Mmm-hmm." Omar noticed another couple wiggling sandwich triangles at a skinny, black dog.

"The Mrs. tell me your father was a white-man. A doctor or something. That's true?"

"A turtle scientist," Omar corrected, as the dog inched closer to the couple. For the briefest moment, Omar considered going further and sharing Josephine's nancy story: how Jacob had been "serious about the environment" and had come to Matura to open an eco-resort; how she'd worked there as a cleaner; how after six years Jacob had gotten fed-up with Trinidad; how he'd left them for Dutch Guiana "to help save the Amazon".

But Omar didn't want to talk about Jacob. Especially after the things Josephine had said this morning when she'd slid the picture-frame across the kitchen-table.

"Ma, why you giving me this thing?" Omar had asked, pitching his spoon down as if a lump of shit had surfaced in his porridge bowl.

"Because you is a big man now, but you turning out just like your father: selfish and ungrateful. Take this, put it up in your room in Pleasantview and watch it good every day. Tell yourself you will be better than him, son. That you will be a real man, the kind that does sacrifice and mind his family. All these years, I do my best for you; now is your turn to work. Now, get your long, bony, backside up and go."

The stray dog finally nuzzled the bread.

"Scientist, eh?" Mr. Jagroop warbled, through a clump of sno-cone. "I is a nature-lover myself, you know. I always say one day me and Mannie go drive up, like big-time tourist, and do some turtle-watching. But work, Omar. Work is a bitch."

Omar felt a tiny flicker of superiority. *He* had seen the famous leatherback turtles a million times. He had proof right there in his bag. He felt generous, like a quick glimpse was—at last—something *he* could gift to Mr. Jagroop. He unzipped the duffel and felt for the square edges of the picture frame. He drew it out, from the T-shirt he'd used as padding. The picture frame was unbroken. The photo was intact.

"Look, Mr. Jagroop. Look a leatherback."

Mr. Jagroop glanced down at Omar's lap and almost choked on the ice. "Waaaaay!" he said, "That thing real fuckin' big! And who's that wooly-head boy with no front teeth there?"

Omar smiled. "Me." There he was, a grinning six-year-old with blondish-brown curls, tiny beside the turtle.

"And that's your daddy? That's why you so fair and your eye-them so orange?"

Jacob knelt on the other side, glaring at the camera. Yes, they did have the same fiery brown eyes.

Without answering, Omar tried to shove the picture back into the bag.

But Mr. Jagroop grabbed his wrist, still marveling. "Watch how you kneel down there like you ain't even frighten!"

"I wasn't frighten," Omar snapped.

"Humph! Well, you better than me, son." Mr. Jagroop patted Omar's hand, then released him with a promise, "When we ready to make that north coast trip, you is the first man we calling."

Omar softened, once more. "Anytime, Mr. Jagroop, anytime."

He re-wrapped the picture frame. Maybe it had been a good idea to show it, after all. Maybe Josephine was right: you have to put out some of yourself, show some of yourself, if you want people to like you.

The truck stopped.

Omar cracked open the door and slid himself out from under the duffel bag.

Mr. Jagroop called after him, "Don't stay long, eh. I waiting."

The pink bungalow was easy to find. Its casement windows were spread wide. Its teak double-doors—the color of healthy, tanned skin—spread even wider. Hot-pink bougainvillea blossoms quivered to the tock-tock of wafting Latin music, and the aroma of boiled rice—sticky and warm—enticed Omar.

He let himself into the yard. By the time he reached the doorway, a wrinkled Chinese woman was standing there, arms akimbo. She wore a house-dress so thinned by washing Omar could see her yellow panties and could tell she had no breasts. She picked her teeth with a matchstick and asked, "Who you come for, li'l boy?"

While he wiggled the envelope from his jeans, Omar explained he'd been sent by Mr. Jagroop to Ms. Lee Loy, the Boss Lady. The woman snatched the packet, then swung her face toward the open door and screeched, "Consuela! Your man really send the thing, girl! Like he desperate."

Omar heard furniture shifting and heels hitting the wooden floor.

The Chinese lady licked her thumb and began counting notes. Three women appeared in the doorway, cluck-clucking among themselves. They all wore makeup and party clothes. But the one who caught Omar's attention was tiny and had the whitest skin he'd ever seen—whiter than his, maybe as white as his father's—paper-white, making the bruise around her eye seem like the imprint of an ink bottle. She prattled—bad English with lots of rolling *R*s—just like the Venezuelan fishermen who docked at Matura from time to time.

Omar guessed this was "Consuela". He stared at her

damaged face while Boss Lady counted the thousands, and the women watched the envelope as if they expected it might become a dove and fly away.

Mr. Jagroop barely uttered a syllable for the rest of the drive. He seemed to sink into a private pool of worry, his face taking on that look Omar had glimpsed earlier in the hammock. And now there was another face on Omar's mind: Consuela's; her blue-black eye. Omar couldn't forget it. Who had hit her? Was the money for that? He stared out the windscreen, puzzling. Ever so often, though, he stole sideways glances at Mr. Jagroop. Was he the one?

When they stopped in front of the house on Mungal Trace, the old man finally spoke. "Thanks eh, son. But let we keep this between weself, nah? She don't bound to know." Mr. Jagroop flicked his eyes toward the upper flat, making it clear he was referring to his wife.

Omar made to get out of the truck but, at the last moment, turned back and shut the door. He needed to confirm what had just happened, what he'd just been a part of. He could only think of one delicate way to pry. "That place, Mr. Jagroop. The pink house. What they does there?" He hoped Mr. Jagroop would say something like "hairdressing" but, at the same time, Omar knew if Mr. Jagroop said that, he wouldn't believe. There was a similar house in Matura—whole day, the women just sat on the porch, all dolled-up, waiting. Omar knew what went on there because Josephine had threatened to chop off his legs if he ever set foot on that porch. What would she think of him now?

Mr. Jagroop lowered his voice as if someone else was in the truck. "Boy, Mannie get he-self in a li'l problem, nah. With the Vene girl working there. He was only looking for a li'l fun, but he have a temper when he drink. He hit she, I know it wrong. But . . . is my son."

Mr. Jagroop's eyes seemed to be pleading with Omar to spare him further explanation. It was like seeing the old man naked. Too embarrassing; and, in the truck's cab, they were suddenly too close. Omar stuttered, "Is okay, Mr. Jagroop. I wouldn't say nothing. I understand," as he cranked the door handle. He jumped down and watched the truck driving away, its trail of black diesel smoke tentacling behind, filling Omar's nostrils and reaching down his throat, making him hawk and spit into the drain.

He opened the gate and, from upstairs, came the explosive *hiss-ss-ss!* of Mrs. Jagroop throwing something into hot oil—a better smell: curry powder, onion, garlic and pepper—and then the rhythmic clang of metal on metal, spoon on pot. He used the noise as a cloak to get to his room, unnoticed by her. Did she know what a brute her precious son was?

Inside, Omar eased the duffel from his sore shoulder and felt as if he'd been travelling for years to get to this moment. He slid the picture frame onto the dresser and, immediately, the Jagroops evaporated from his thoughts. He clawed at the red welts the bag had left on his shoulder and felt his body itching everywhere, somewhere he couldn't quite reach, as he stared into the photo.

"Now what?" he mumbled, daring some invisible opponent. Through the patchwork of greasy little fingerprints on the glass, Omar tried to see something, feel something positive about the picture. Josephine had always kept it in the secret depths of her wardrobe. She'd take it out on his birthday and allow Omar to study it and ask as many questions as he liked. But three years ago, on his fourteenth birthday, Omar had told her not to bother. His questions had deepened over time, and her thready answers—"I don't know . . . I not sure . . . Your father never said . . ."—could no longer span the yawning gaps in his mind. Was Jacob alive or dead? Did Omar show up in his dreams the way he did in Omar's? Did he wake up crying, too? Or did he belong to a new family now?

Vapors of a painful—but familiar, unnameable—emotion began to rise inside Omar. He fled the picture and flung himself onto the bed. He reached across the nightstand for a half-eaten pack of peanuts and a half-empty Coke that didn't even fizz anymore. He poured both down his throat, sat up and looked around. It was barely midday but the tiny room was stifling due to the thick, red curtains Mrs. Jagroop had hung over the chicken-wire window. He wanted to tie up the curtains—but then he'd have no privacy. He wanted to turn on a TV, a radio—something loud, louder than his thoughts—but he had nothing.

Omar couldn't stop his eyes; they returned to the photo. Ha! There was one good thing about it: it had helped him make friends with Mr. Jagroop. A fresh wave of disgust for Mannie swept over Omar. It wasn't fair: big, black Mannie had hit that tiny, perfect, white doll; and Mr. Jagroop was cleaning up the mess. Shelling out big, big money. On one hand, Omar couldn't blame him; that's what a father should do: protect his son. But Mannie didn't deserve such a father. And furthermore, Consuela didn't deserve to be treated like that. Mannie would never have gotten off so easy with a local girl—they had brothers, fathers, people of their own kind to defend them. The whole thing was so unfair.

Omar swung his feet to the floor and covered his face with his hands. This weird feeling overtook him sometimes—more and more since leaving school. His skin was scorching. Palms upturned, he examined his forearms. Veins stood out, thick and blue, and he thought he could see each one throbbing. It looked like Life. So much Life. And Energy. And Power. Power, blue like electricity. Power searching for an outlet or a route to ground. Too much for him to contain. It made his eyes bulge. It made his temples pulse. It made a crackling noise in his ears and it made his heart hurt. What to do with all this Life? Some days, like today, it all backed up inside of him and Omar felt he would explode.

He was seventeen years old. Six months ago he was swinging a lunch-bag in the schoolyard. Now, he was alone. His mother kept saying he was "a big man now". But a man was powerful and did things with his power—things *he* wanted to do, not what other people made him do. Omar sprung up and began pacing the room, berating himself: he should have stood up to Josephine this morning; he shouldn't have let her force him into coming back here, or bringing the picture; he shouldn't have lingered at Mr. Jagroop's store, or let himself be pressured into doing that favor—into ganging up against someone with no one on her side.

Then, Omar had a thought that made his stomach even more queasy: what if Mr. Jagroop didn't really like him? All that talk in the truck: about trusting Omar; saying they would call him one day to show them around the north coast. What if Mr. Jagroop was only mamaguying him to drop off the money?

Omar rushed to the dresser and, before he could even stop himself, he'd punched its side. The cardboard panel flexed, wobbled, then fell out. That wasn't enough for the force moving inside him. He lunged toward the bathroom and felt a *whoosh!* through his veins as he struck the hollow bathroom door, heard the crunching of the thin plywood, felt the shock to his knuckles and the bright, red satisfaction of his fist emerging through the other side. Omar removed his arm slowly and inspected the splinters in his hand. No pain. Just relief, and a kind of pride, as he noticed the hole he'd made was so much bigger than his fist.

A voice. It reached Omar as if he were underwater. Then an impatient sound—*blam, blam, blam*—fishermen pushing off, knocking the side of a pirogue. He startled awake. Someone was banging on his door.

It was now dark outside. Through the chicken-wire, under a low-swinging bulb, he saw Mr. Jagroop, Mannie, Dev and his father, Mr. Singh. They sat on crates, crouched over a small table, eating.

When Omar opened the door, Mr. Jagroop dumped a big dollop of curry onto a plate and pointed to the roti they were using to cradle the bony pieces of meat and sop up the sauce.

"Boy, come sit down," he ordered. "You from the country; you must like wild meat."

Omar remained in the doorway, crusty-eyed and

slack-jawed until Mr. Jagroop beckoned again. Only then did Omar peel himself from the doorframe and accept the plate. He didn't know what else to do. Everyone was staring at him.

He popped a morsel into his mouth and chewed slowly, assessing the meat: iguana. In Matura, they were everywhere, like chickens. Silence seemed to hum around the table and Omar knew the men were waiting for him to show some manners, to compliment the food.

"In Matura we does curry 'guana," he half-whispered, "but it don't taste nice so."

Everyone nodded and Mr. Jagroop credited Mannie and Dev for catching the animals.

"You does hunt, Omar?" Mannie asked.

Omar took time clearing his teeth, calculating his reply. He felt disoriented. Was he really sitting here among these men? Had they really come seeking him? Mr. Jagroop must've told them how he'd helped earlier today. They were all trying with him now, he had to try too, the way Josephine had said.

"Hunt?" he answered at last. "Yeah. I used to go in the forest with them fellas. Catch we li'l wild-meat. Do we li'l fishing and thing."

Everyone grinned and swapped looks that Omar couldn't read. He'd only ever been on one job interview—at Save-U—but this felt very similar. Eventually, Mr. Singh blurted out, "Well all these months we watching you—quiet, quiet; going home every weekend; avoiding everybody. We say you is a born-again-Christian. Judgey, nah. Ain't, Jagroop? But we ain't know you is a real man—a hunting man."

One by one, the men stretched across: Mr. Jagroop clapped

Omar's back, Mr. Singh slapped his knee, Mannie and Dev fist-bumped his shoulder. Then, as if a switch had been flipped, the mood lightened and the men all chattered at once, competing for attention.

Omar found himself in the middle of a lime.

Mr. Singh drew a flask of puncheon rum from his pocket and said, "Let we finish this." They passed it around and, when it reached Omar, the group fell silent again, watching him. Omar hated rum, but he wanted them to see he wasn't "judgey" so he tipped the tiniest bit into his cup, then drowned it with coconut water. The men roared with laughter. "Good one, good one," they said, slapping him on the back again. But they skipped over him the next time the flask went around. They understood him now, Omar thought. He was a quiet fella but would never stop anybody else from having their fun. It made him wonder; maybe he'd read them wrong as well. Except Mannie, of course; that jackass who'd hit Consuela and jeopardized his hardworking father. Omar would never like Mannie, but maybe he could tolerate him—for Mr. Jagroop's sake. Plus, Josephine had said, "Try."

"Omar, bring the picture, nah?" Mr. Jagroop asked. "I was trying to explain these fellas 'bout that turtle, but is best you show them the real thing."

Omar sprinted to his room and returned with the picture-frame.

The group *ooh-ed* and *ahh-ed* as it made the rounds. Then they asked stupid questions, like whether turtles have teeth; if they bite people.

Omar's answers were brief at first, but every time he spoke, he felt a strong current—pulling something from them to him—making swirls and eddies inside him. He was winning the men's attention and, he suspected, their respect. This kind of power was new to Omar and it rippled through the cavern of his belly like a new hunger. He leaned forward on his plastic crate, tapping the picture as he talked and talked. He shared all he knew about turtles—anatomy, habitat, seasons—everything.

When the lecture ended, there was a pocket of silence as every man contemplated the floor. Then, Mr. Jagroop punched his thigh and said, "Well, I ready to go Matura!" He pointed around the table and everyone else agreed. "It settle then. Saturday night, we turtle-watching. And Omar, *you* go be we leader."

Omar was dotish for the next five days, as if Mr. Jagroop had uttered an obeah spell instead of a mere promise. At night in his bedroom, and by day at Save-U, Omar relived the high points of the lime—the way he'd taught the men, their admiring looks—and he imagined further ways he could impress them on Saturday's excursion.

On Tuesday, Save-U was in the usual mid-morning lull when Omar decided to fix the most important item for Saturday: a turtle-friendly torch. From the Home Goods lane he got a flashlight and some duct tape, from the stand with gift bags and wrapping-paper he got a red cellophane sheet, and from his cashier, Cindy, he got some batteries. While she prattled on with the neighboring cashier, Omar sat on his stool rigging the torch, taping and testing to make sure it would only emit red light—enough for the men to see the turtles, but not so much as to harm the animals. He was engrossed until Cindy banged the counter and said, "Customer." When he looked up, Consuela was standing there at his register, waiting for her yogurt, deodorant and maxi-pads to be bagged.

Omar dropped the torch and began fumbling for a plastic bag.

"Sorry," Cindy said, "this one does move slow."

"Is okay," Consuela answered, "I know him."

At that, Omar's head jerked and he finally met her eyes. She was as white and as beautiful as he remembered; the bruises were almost invisible—except to him, maybe. A red blouse partially covered her breasts and she wore red leggings topped with a thick gold belt. The belt had been pulled so tight it made her exposed midriff look like one of the corn muffins made at the in-store bakery. Omar dropped his head again and fussed with the yogurt.

"You did went by the house," Consuela said, her voice loud in the quiet of Save-U.

It was an accusation and Omar was sure his co-workers had heard. The tips of his ears and his neck were on fire; red enough, he guessed, for everybody to see his guilt. He picked up the deodorant and felt himself grow even redder at the thought that this was how Consuela smelled: Powder Fresh. Then came the feminine products. As Omar handled Consuela's maxi-pads, his prick began inflating and unfolding itself like a life raft. And because he didn't understand why, when all he really felt for her was pity, he shoved the bags across the counter and turned away.

"You es no a very nice person," she said. "Just like *tu Papa*, Jagroop."

The rest of the week passed and Omar never told Mr. Jagroop about that incident. Instead, on mornings, he helped the old man load the trucks. On evenings, Mrs. Jagroop came downstairs to hand Omar a plate of roti and talkari, a home-cooked meal. And on Thursday night, after she'd left, Mannie appeared at Omar's chicken-wire window, head bent like a timid stray.

"I just come to say thanks, nah. For helping Daddy. You save he ass, there."

Omar was tempted to say, "Is *your* ass I save! Stop hiding behind your father," but something about Mannie's sheepish face made Omar hold his tongue.

They were almost the same age. Boys. Boys made mistakes.

In one week, Omar had moved from wasting in no-man's-land to feeding on the fringe of this family, and he was determined that, after Saturday night, he'd have a permanent place among them.

Mannie parked the truck along a dirt road they would never have found without Omar. Then came a sloping embankment covered in thorny bushes. Their bare arms and legs would've been shredded if Omar hadn't walked ahead, swiping a long cut-lass. Then, they stepped out onto a deserted beach that stretched for miles in either direction. Everything was blue-black, making it difficult to distinguish between sand, sea and sky. There was a moon, peeking out behind a buttress of clouds, and the ocean was at full, angry volume.

"This way," Omar said. He led them past a crowd of coconut trees, shifting in the night breeze, as if uneasy at the sudden appearance of the men. Like a good host, he pointed to some fallen nuts and promised that, on the way back, he would chop some so they could have fresh coconut water before driving back to Pleasantview.

For a long time, mostly in silence, the men trudged behind. Then, Mr. Jagroop caught up to Omar. Panting and wheezing, he whispered, "Ahhm . . . you see that thing you drop off the other day? It looking like every week, boy. You don't mind?"

Omar felt himself cringe and then stiffen, as if he'd collected a basketball to the stomach. So it wasn't over: the whore-house; the hush-money. Every week? No way. He couldn't do it. And he had no good reason except that it made him feel as if he were right there, watching Mannie hit Consuela and then handing him a towel to wipe his knuckles. Plus, he didn't want to see her again, couldn't bear her accusing eyes. He would only go to Consuela again if he could be her white knight. But how? He was just a helpless boy.

"Well, I . . . " His Adam's apple bobbed, but he didn't have the words to refuse Mr. Jagroop. He squinted into the blackness ahead, searching, desperate now for some sign of a turtle. Anybody could carry an envelope but only *he* could give Mr. Jagroop a turtle, up close. This, he could offer him this; maybe it would be enough.

There! Omar stopped everyone and pointed to a dark blur in the distance, midway between the tree-line and the water. He hurried to investigate and then scampered back, waving for the men to follow. They climbed and picked their way along the theatre-like curve of a rock cluster. He took the torch from his pocket, aimed it at the sand below.

Dev snickered, "W'happen Omar? Like you carrying we in the red-light district, or what?

Omar shushed him and continued tracing an outline with the torch till their eyes adjusted and the men recognized what lay beneath them.

There, resembling a big rock itself, was a leatherback turtle.

At least six feet long, almost as wide, with white specks lining its dark brown skin. Under the red light, it appeared buffed and polished for this big reveal. Its head was about two feet long. Its giant flippers sloshed back and forth, making a sand angel. Omar explained that the animal had finished covering its eggs and was now heading back to the ocean.

For the next few minutes, the group sat spellbound—even Omar. For him, something was different this time. Maybe he was seeing the turtle through the strangers' eyes? Or maybe *he* was different? Not just the scientist's son anymore, but an expert in his own right—a teacher of other men. He watched the animal's head poking in and out, hesitant. The creature seemed less powerful than he remembered; more vulnerable, lonely. If poachers came up on this beach right now, nobody could help it. Nobody. The poor thing was driven by this instinct to return to the beach where it was born, to lay its eggs in the same place, to come back home. But what if home is no longer safe?

The spell wore off. The men came to terms with the turtle's proportions. It lost all its wonder. Mr. Singh suggested, "Pictures, pictures," and the group scrambled down the rocks like children on a field trip.

"No, no. Stay behind it," Omar called, but nobody listened.

Dev dug a video camera from his backpack and handed it to Omar with a few cursory instructions and an order, "Film we."

Omar felt uneasy. Still, he stabbed the cutlass into the damp sand, took a few steps back, pointed the torch and began filming.

At first, the men knelt around the turtle at respectful distances. Then they edged closer. When Mr. Jagroop touched the creature's back, a competition started: Mr. Singh patted the head; Dev held a flipper, trying to wave it at the camera. Mannie sat on the turtle; Dev pushed him off and lay down. The young men began a war of poses atop the turtle while their fathers applauded and flicked away hysterical tears.

Omar wanted to say something: leatherbacks didn't have hard shells; the men might be hurting the animal. But he kept thinking it would be over any minute now, that it was just a little harmless fun. Soon, the men did run out of clever poses and Omar was relieved that he hadn't made a big deal.

He needed to play his cards right tonight. If he did, it wouldn't matter so much when he told Mr. Jagroop he couldn't be their whorehouse bag-man anymore. He would help at the store, with the truck, around the house, even; but he couldn't help with that other problem.

The men were circling the turtle like they were at a car show. Omar decided this was a convenient moment to capture the full scenery. He panned the camera left, to the water; up, at the moon; then, a slow three-sixty: mountains, coconut trees, rocks; then he was back at the group. Mr. Singh and Dev were at the front of the turtle, Mr. Jagroop and Mannie were behind. The four men struggled for a grip on the creature as they attempted to move it.

"Aye! What allyuh doing? Stop! Stop!" Omar cried, running toward them.

They straightened, chests heaving. Dev said, "Boy, put down the camera and come help we."

Mannie said, "Nah, we can't lift this. Not even with Omar. This thing had to be about five hundred pounds. Let we just forget it."

"Not a fuck of that!" Mr. Singh argued, "I hear turtle is the sweetest fish-meat you will ever eat. I ain't come so far, this hour in the night, to go back without a li'l piece! Is only two flippers we need—look how they big." He kicked one for emphasis. "We could chop them off just so."

Omar's heart raced. "Mr. Jagroop," he pleaded, looking to the old man to thwart Singh.

In a stern voice, Mr. Jagroop said, "Singh, I is a nature-lover. We can't do the animal that."

"Exactly!" Omar said.

Then, Mr. Jagroop continued, "We have to put it to sleep first. I think we could get a clean lash from here. Pass me the cutlass. In fact, give Omar. He is the turtle man. He go know where the jugular is."

Mannie plucked the cutlass from the sand and inclined the handle toward Omar.

Omar accepted it, shivering with the unwelcome understanding that he'd reached the end of something—everything—and the beginning of something else . . . what?

He saw himself raise the cutlass to heaven and throw back his head. He saw it as if he wasn't doing it. He saw himself lowering the cutlass toward the turtle. He saw a single dark line. But then midway, at shoulder level, he saw silver: moon, glinting on the blade's edge. A simple rotation of the wrist and now the cutlass was no longer aimed at the animal, but slanted toward Mannie.

Omar let out a guttural noise—surprising, even to him— and began swinging the cutlass wildly. "Nah! Nah! Not tonight! Nobody touching this fuckin' turtle tonight! You hear me! No-fuckin'-body!"

Mr. Singh and Dev leapt in one direction, Mr. Jagroop and Mannie in the other. And, as Omar advanced, they hopped backward, saying things like, "Aye! Cunt-hole, relax nah!"

"Noooo! Allyuh have to pass through me first!" Omar kept screaming. "Through motherfuckin'-me!"

Mannie made to challenge Omar with a piece of driftwood but, with one chop, the branch split. At that, the men turned and ran.

Omar chased them clear past the rocks and out onto the open beach. He would've gone further too, but he fell—his body going one way, cutlass the next. He staggered up, found it and began to hack at the sand. Needing to damage something, he ran to the nearest tree and began to chop at the nuts underneath. But they mostly rolled away, evading him.

He took a mighty swing at the tree, and shuddered as the blade imbedded itself.

All energy drained from him. He had none left to remove the cutlass. He backed away, crying, and sank to his knees.

They'd tricked him. Made him believe he was bringing them turtle-watching, when all along they'd planned a hunt. Made him believe *he* could belong with *them*. He hated the men for raising his hopes. He hated himself for believing. And he hated Mr. Jagroop most of all. For not being the man he expected him to be. For being the kind of man who asked a boy to do his dirty work. For being the kind of man who could kill a defenseless leatherback turtle. A mother that had just laid eggs. If Mr. Jagroop could do that, what else could he do?

Omar decided he was never going back to the Jagroops, to Pleasantview. Not that night, not ever. He would remain right here, he would stay home.

Then, he remembered the picture frame.

He shut his tired eyes and saw it there, face up, in the tomb of his bottom drawer. He knew the photo by heart, all its details: his face, innocent and open; Jacob's, closed against the world. Maybe he should go back for it? Maybe Jacob had been a better man than Jagroop all along. A worse father, yes; but maybe a better man.

These were Omar's watery, receding thoughts, as his eyelids succumbed to fatigue, and a clump of sand rolled from his slackening fist. He spent the night there, next to the rocks, just another blue-black mound between the tree line and the Matura sea.

White Envelope

I IN THE KITCHEN, SETTING THE table, when I hear Mr. H open the front door. I hear when the li'l metal feet on his briefcase touch the coffee table. I hear the fabric rustle when he pass through the brocade dividing the front room and bedroom; and then I hear the *click-clacking* when he pass through the beaded curtain into the kitchen. Now he grabbing my waist and biting my neck. "You good to put in house, girl!" he saying. And I giggling, the way I's always react whenever he trying to sound like he from 'round here, from Pleasantview. Still, the moment he mention putting me in house, my heart start flapping like a hummingbird wing. I can't wait to tell him the news. My mother say I shouldn't say nothing; but she wrong—she don't know the man like how I know him.

I start dishing out the food and I feeling Mr. H eyes following every which way I turn. He love me, I know it, he does always tell me. And I love him too, in a kinda way. I mean, it hard not to feel sorry for him: the poor man been living a lie he whole life. Except when he here with me. Early o'clock he did tell me the whole story 'bout he and he wife, Joan The Witch. When he was twenty, the marriage get arrange but, because all the money did come from *she* side, she family treat him like a dog. He stick it out for the children, though. And now, the only reason is because he and The Witch so tangle-up in the cloth business. "Divorces are rare in the Syrian community," Mr. H does say, "it's simply bad for business." But he been putting some money away—for years now—and one day soon he should have enough to say, "Fuck it!" and start a new store and a new life. After all, he only fifty-nine, he always saying. Mr. H come just like me: longing for a new life bad, bad, bad.

I rest down the spaghetti and ruffle the li'l semi-circle of hair he still have. I watch him make the Sign of the Cross and then he start attacking the food. He does come 'round once or twice a week and, every time, I does make sure and cook something from that Italian recipe book. The one I did borrow from work and photocopy after he did say how much he love pasta. Poor thing: Joan don't cook, and all he does get home is maid food.

Slapping the plastic tablecloth now, he bawl, "My God, Gail! This Bolognese is divine." Then he keep on smiling and watching me over the wine glass while we eating. I want to tell him, I want to tell him, but I know is better to wait till he finish the food and the wine and he in a nice mellow mood.

"You're really improving with those . . . the cutlery," he say. "Almost natural." But he don't know how I did beg my friend, Crystal, to teach me to eat with knife-and-fork; and how much I does practice when I here by myself. I want Mr. H to see I could learn new things, I could blend in good with his lifestyle. Just because I start off in Pleasantview don't mean I bound to stay here.

Now, he swallowing the last mouthful. "Well, boy am I glad

I came straight here," he say. "I hate keeping all that cash from the store on me—especially in this neck of the woods—but I was starving and this was excellent, darling."

I pour Mr. H a second glass of wine—is his favorite. The name on a paper in my wallet, just in case I ever have to ask somebody in the grocery. But sometimes, while I brushing my teeth, I does pout in the mirror and practice it in a sexy voice: "Bow-jho-lay".

He loosen his pants button and push back from the table. He patting his knee. "Come here," he say, "that meal deserves a kiss." He licking the last drop of sauce from the crease of his mouth. His tongue and teeth red too, from the wine, and when he flash a broad smile and pull me down in his lap, I don't know why but my mind run on Dracula.

I let Mr. H shift me 'round to make room for his pot-belly. "You putting on a little weight?" he ask. He did say the same thing last week but I didn't take the test then, so I didn't want to jinx nothing by talking before I was sure, sure, sure. Now I certain.

"Yeah," I giggle, "and is all your fault." I start stroking his scaly white scalp and kissing his forehead. My child-father, my child-father. Look how far we come, nah. Look how I manage to turn things 'round from where we did start off.

Last year, when I did just get the cashier job in Textile Kingdom, the first impression I did have of my boss, Mr. H, was that he look like a hunchback from the movies. Ugly: short, squat, with pudgy, hairy hands and I could tell the rest of him was cover-up in the same coarse hair. It had a day I went in his office to collect the cash-drawer to start my shift. When he grab me and pull me so, on top his bulging crotch, I was really surprise—I nearly bawl out. But by the time he wrap his hand in my hair and drag my face down to his, I realize what was coming. I let him have my mouth. And when his tarantula-looking hand crawl up under my skirt, although I did stiffen up with fright, I didn't push it away. And when he bend me over the desk, I just bite my lip and grip on the edge till it feel like the skin over my knuckles was busting open. Yes, I small in body; but I bear that man weight and I never flinch. I did switch-off. I was picturing my mother, Janice, and hearing the advice she did give me the day I leave high school: "Listen, you is a sexy girl; any man go want what you have between your leg. Put a price-tag on it and find a man who could pay that. Don't be stupid like me and waste your life on no Pleasantview man." And I was already thinking I would let Mr. H to do this thing again. And again. And again. No matter how he ugly. No matter how it hurting. And I was telling myself is not rape if I could make him pay me for what he take. Make him give me a new life outside Pleasantview.

I take a deep breath and push the air up my nose-hole, up inside my head, trying to push out the memory of that first, scary time. With the air come Mr. H smell: cigar and dusty cloth. It don't usually bother me but tonight it upsetting my stomach. I hear that does happen to some women in this early stage.

He nuzzling my neck, rubbing my back, teasing in his Pleasantview accent, "Is too much nice life. Ain't?"

Yes, Mr. H truly, truly give me a nice life over the last year. Soon after that first time in the office, he did make me throw out my room-mate, Crystal, and he start paying the full rent here. Then, Joan The Witch did find out 'bout us so she fire me from Textile Kingdom. Mr. H lie down next to me, that very same night, tracing the star-shape birthmark on my leg. He say, "When I was your age I wanted to be an architect. I designed my house, you know."

"For true? It nice, man," I did say.

Turning on his elbow and stroking my face, he ask me, "What you wanted to be when you were a little girl?"

"A chef," I did say.

"Yes, I should've guessed." He smile and say, "You do love to cook."

Two days after that talk, Mr. H pick me up—not in the big Benz that Vishnu, the chauffeur, does drive; but in the smaller one *he* does drive himself—and he take me to meet the Wallaces, the people who own the snackette where I working now. "You will be safe with Uncle as your boss," Mr. H did say. "He is eighty-something. Too old to pull at you. But if he tries it, let me know."

For Carnival, Mr. H parade me, like a beauty-queen, through the VVIP Section of almost every big-shot party. Then, for Easter we went to that hotel in Tobago, where all the foreign white-people does go. Parasail, snorkel—man, I do all kinda thing Joan The Witch never do with the man. "I forgot how to feel like this," Mr. H did say when we was walking the beach one evening. "She stole my best years. But you, Gail, you've given me back my youth." And for my birthday, just last month, Mr. H give me a ring. Custom-made by his jeweler, he say. A single garnet solitaire—my birthstone—it look like the most perfect drop of blood just happen to land on a circle of twenty-four-karat gold. When he slip it on my finger, he say, "I wish this were a diamond. But one day it will be, my darling."

All this in my mind now, as I sitting down here in his lap, and I feeling so excited. No more stepping over shit-smelling drains, no more bullets popping all hours of the night, no more wondering when the garbage truck will pass, no more feeling shame to write my address on a form. Me and my child go be up the hill, on a quiet street, playing on a green, green lawn and just waiting for Daddy to come home from his new store. I will have a proper family. Which woman in Pleasantview have that? No running-down man and showing up on man job to cuss for pampers and milk—none of that for me. I have Mr. H and he have me and we going after that new life, starting tonight. With both hands, I gather up Mr. H cheeks till he looking like a big baby. I lock-on to his eyes, like I's a doctor checking for cataract.

"I pregnant," I say. "Eight weeks."

Them eyes get wide, and wider, and wider still; then suddenly they smaller than ever—a squint. He shaking off my touch the way a dog does shed water. "You're kidding?"

"No. I very serious." I grinning still, watching him like how people does watch for eclipse.

But then Mr. H jump up and start pacing the kitchen, questions clattering the air like fireworks. "When did you find out? Have you been to the doctor? Who have you told besides me?"

I was expecting this kinda interrogation and walking 'round, like if he name Matlock. Oh God, this man could be so dramatic sometimes! I answer everything—calm, calm with a li'l smirk—because I know that's his way: he can't listen unless he know every single detail.

Finally, Mr. H stop wearing out my rubber-tiles—"linoleum", he does call it. He sit down, pulling the chair closer till our knees touching, then he sandwich my hands as if we praying the Act of Contrition—like he does sometimes insist after we done make love. The white, crinkly leather on his face shaping-up a smile. In a tender whisper he say, "Not to worry, my darling. We'll solve this. I have a guy. Best in class. He's quick and discreet. I promise: you won't feel a pinch."

A cramping start up in my belly. I want to pull away but Mr. H have my fingers lace-up with his.

He saying, "I'll even go with you . . . I'll be right there . . ."

The cramping turn into a stabbing—a inside-out stabbing. I understand exactly what the man saying, but I don't understand *why* he saying it. I start crying and I hear every sentence coming out the same way, "But you say . . . But you say . . . Ain't you say . . ." But Mr. H have a plaster for every sore tonight: he too old; he can't get divorced because of the business; he don't have enough money put away.

"But you say is a fresh start you want. Together. So you would never have to go back to that big, lonely house . . . Ain't you say you have so much regrets? That you wish you did married somebody like me? That you wish you could go back and be a better father? You don't remember? This is what we been talking about, this is our dream!"

"Good God, Gail! Don't be such a child! Think. Do you know what would happen if people pursued every silly dream they ever had?"

I run to the bedroom, my panty-drawer—the place I does keep everything important—and I pull out the li'l cardboard box with the garnet ring. I push it right up in Mr. H face. "What happen to this? Eh? You did wish it was a diamond. We have a good reason now."

The man skin-up he nose like I is something dead in the road. "Clearly, I've put too much faith in you, Gail. Don't you grasp the difference between birthday tidings and a marriage proposal?"

I pelt the ring box and watch it bounce off he greasy forehead.

Well, is now the man get vicious! Spitting venom like a frighten cobra: "What the hell were you thinking? Why didn't you protect yourself? Are you trying to trap me?"

Trap? Like he forget: *I* used to buy the pills and take them . . . most days . . . nobody perfect. And is *I* used to beg him to be careful, to wear a rubbers; but it had so much times he did get carried away, bawling how he need it skin-to-skin. So, how he could blame me? I didn't plan this. This is God work.

I trying to tell Mr. H these things, but it useless. I never yet see him get-on so. All of a sudden he like a raving monster— not the nice hunchback—a real monster. And he just twisting everything, ripping through our whole relationship and I don't know what magic words go make him turn back into the prince I know. I double-over in the chair and start bawling my liver-string out.

"Shut up! Before your neighbors hear," Mr. H say. And I try. I really, really try. I clamp my own hand over my own mouth, until the only noise coming out is the kind you does hear sick people making in the hospital. No, no, how he could do me this? How?

Mr. H ain't saying nothing. But his face the color it does be after sex and his lips is a tight, white line. Outta the corner of my eye, I watch him leave the kitchen and walk through the bedroom—past the king-size bed he did buy for Christmas—to the front room where his briefcase is.

I have this twitch—like a false-start in the blocks—to run behind him. But I don't hear the door so I wait. I tell myself he just cooling down. He rethinking all the nasty things he just say. He regretting them. He feeling shame. "Is okay," I tell him in my mind. "Just come back. I forgive you. We have a family to think 'bout."

Mr. H back now, holding a white envelope and a piece of note-paper with a raggedy edge where it tear off. Like a TV magician with a pack of cards, he bring the envelope down, eye-level, and start flicking a pile of hundred-dollar bills. Then, he fold-up the note-paper and tuck it behind the cash. In a deadly tone he say, "Gail, I will not step foot in this apartment until you call this doctor and make the arrangements. You have a month. Then, I stop paying rent."

With that, Mr. H gone.

Four hours later, I still by the table. Is like when you trying to wake up from a nightmare but you can't move—like something holding you down—and you can't scream neither. Every time I look at this damn envelope I know it was real. But then what was fake? Everything I ever hear him say? Everything I ever see in his eyes? No! I not crazy, I didn't make it up. Nobody could lie so good. Fake real tears? No! It must be something I do wrong tonight: I choose the wrong words maybe.

Or maybe *you* just wrong, a voice in my head pipe-up.

Maybe Janice was right. She did warn me not to tell Mr. H I pregnant. She did come out and say it plain, plain, "Girl, if you know what side your bread butter on, you will throw-way that child and keep your man. It too early for that. You ain't really get nothing much from he yet. Make him mind you till you get house and car and your bank-book fat. Then you could take the risk."

I did get vex when Janice tell me that. "I shoulda know you would say so," I did tell her. "Children was always disposable for you. Like maxi-pad, ain't?"

It wasn't a nice thing to say. Every Friday night, my father, Luther Senior, used to come home drunk, beat her and then cry, "Oh Gawwwd! Ah love yuh, Janice! Why you does make me have to beat you for? Eh? Why, Janice?" One night, after he beat she till she face twist, she move out and leave we. I was twelve, Luther Junior was seventeen—old enough to know we couldn't really blame her. But still, I woulda never do my children that. I don't want to be like Janice. I not throwing away my child. I want my child to have a proper family.

I go fix this, I have to fix this. It can't end so.

I ain't sleep whole night. The tossing and turning; the crying. And Mr. H words in my head like a record sticking. And his face. Oh God, that face: a white cloud turning grey with rage. I don't understand it. The man give me a whole year of words and feelings and everything heading in one direction and then— *Bam!*—last night: U-turn.

I throw open the top half of my kitchen door. Is only seven, but the sunlight barging in, as if it was waiting on the back-step whole night. Is the kinda heat does make green things turn brown and dead. Through the glare, I peep up by the back-house to see if Miss Ivy windows open yet. I been thinking 'bout her since four o'clock when I did get up to pee.

I need help. I need advice from somebody who know Mr. H longer than me. *Yes!* The windows open and the flowered curtain tie-up in a knot.

On the first knock, Miss Ivy answer. "A-A! Gail, what happen doux-doux? How your face hang down like Tom Dooley so? Something wrong?"

Miss Ivy talking like she surprise but, underneath, I getting a vibes like she was expecting me. It have me uncomfortable and I almost make a excuse to leave, but I don't know nobody else to ask for help. I steady myself and tell Miss Ivy I have a urgent problem so I need her to read the cards and tell me what to do.

"Come in, nah," she say, like she excited.

I sit down on Miss Ivy couch and, almost right away, my thighs start sweating till they glue-down on the clear plastic that covering the cushions. While Miss Ivy knocking pan and kettle in the li'l makeshift kitchen, I take in the whole place. I never been in one of these back-house apartments before. Miss Ivy have it neat and clean but is just one room: only a wobbly fiber-board screen blocking off she jail-style bed; and she does share a toilet with Mr. Winston, the old man living next door. Through the thin paneling I hearing his TV on that Seventh Day Adventist program. I wonder if he might hear what I telling Miss Ivy. But I have worse things to worry about: if I don't change Mr. H mind by month-end, I might be making baby in one of these cardboard-box apartment. Nah! No, Jesus, not my child. Not my half-Syrian child.

Growing up in Pleasantview hard enough if you poor and black; but it worse if you light-skin and have good hair. Then everybody know some high-color man did take your mother for a ass, and that you have a fine, respectable Daddy who don't want you. You come like a double-joke. No, not my child.

Miss Ivy reach back now with the deck of cards she does use to see the future. She rest it down on the wobbly center-table between us. "Give me the full story," she say, "and don't 'fraid to call name."

I start talking and then I start crying but the old lady just sit down there, stoneface, sipping she orange-peel tea. She never once blink and when I done explaining, is me who have to drop my gaze.

"What it is you really want, m'child?" she ask.

"How you mean, Miss Ivy?" I stutter. "God bless me with a child and a child-father who could take we outta Pleasantview. I have a chance for a proper family. I want my family, Miss Ivy."

Resting down her mug, she say, "Gail, doux-doux, God will never bless you with a next woman husband. And I could put my head on a block: He ain't bless you with Mr. H."

"How you could say that, Miss Ivy? You ain't even watch the cards yet and you talking so negative?"

"I don't have to watch the cards to tell you 'bout Mr. H. I clean that man toilet for twenty years. It have nothing I don't know 'bout he. That's why I could tell you, straight to your face, the man is a womanizer. Don't fool yourself—you is not the first."

"Oh, but I is the last, though! I know he had girls before—he confess and tell me all that. But he was just searching. It different with me and him. The connection—it just . . . special. Even he say so."

"Special? Ha, Lord! You think you special, li'l girl? So, you better than all them other li'l girls who did come in here and sit down right where you sitting down to tell me the same story?"

"Yes, Miss Ivy. I make myself different to them. I learn from Mr. H and I try to uplift myself." And it have other reasons I could give her too, reasons why I know me and Mr. H meant to be together. Like how he does hold on to me and cry sometimes, telling me I's the only innocent thing he ever know, I's the only girl who never beg him for money and that's why he trust me with his life. And how he does tell me all his personal business: it hurt him bad, bad that he never had a son; and he does feel guilty 'bout his last daughter, Kimberley—they never get along and he feel that's why she turn lesbian. The man have a hard shell but a melting heart. He grieving for a family—just like me. But I can't tell Miss Ivy all this—is none of she damn business—so she and me just sit down here, watching one another hard.

"M'daughter," she finally sigh—loud, loud—as if she so wise and I so stupid. "You want the child or you don't want the child? Decide your mind. Because you ain't getting the man. Forget that. Soon, he go cut you off and pass you straight like a full bus. Mark my words."

"You was with him, nah?"

"Eh?"

"Talk the truth, Miss Ivy. You fuck Mr. H, ain't?

She not answering and suddenly she can't watch me in my eye. The bitch jealous, oui. Just like Janice. Two old quenk who bitter with how their life turn out so they trying to poison my chance for happiness. I not taking the bait.

A week pass but it feel like a year.

Through it all, I had to try and stay hopeful. I didn't miss a step at work and I never tell nobody my troubles. In fact, I didn't talk much at all; I was busy listening. For Uncle to call my name and hand me a telephone message from Mr. H. For the big Benz to pull-up on the street and for Vishnu to wind down the glass and say, "Come. The Bossman want to see you." At home, for the ring of the phone, the honk of the horn. I was jumpy, jumpy whole week: running, at the sound of every big engine, to peep through the louvres. I never once stop listening—not even in my sleep.

And when I wasn't listening, I was thinking. Geez, I been thinking! Till I get a permanent headache.

But now is Friday morning, start of the second week, and still no sign of Mr. H. I in the bathroom getting ready for work but my mind far. I studying what to do. I didn't rush the man; I give him time to mellow and I give myself time to figure out what I do wrong that night. I was aiming too high, telling Mr. H to leave Joan. That's what scare him: divorce. He frighten 'bout the money, the business. I feel he woulda react different if I did say we coulda just continue how we was going: him visiting, minding me . . . and the child.

I soaping my skin like I trying to rub off the stink of all the things he did say that night. I dip in the bucket, full the old butter container with water and soak down myself. Suds rolling off my body and I lean against the wall, into that clean, clean feeling.

I lock-off the pipe. Decision-time: I calling-in sick. Today, today, I walking up in that cloth-store and facing Mr. H. Not to make a scene or nothing. But to let him know I seeing things different now. He's a proud fella. I's the one who need to make the first move here. And today is a good day for that. Joan don't go in on Fridays—tea-party day. Mr. H will be alone in the store. We go have the office to weself. Miss Ivy say I can't have the child *and* the man. Well, she wrong: with a li'l compromise, I keeping both. And I not leaving Mr. H office until he say, "Go ahead, start looking for a bigger place."

Ten o'clock is the best time to slip in the store without being too noticeable. I leave home at quarter-to and flag down a taxi heading north, to Pleasantview Junction. A straight road and I in the front-seat. For the whole drive, every time I glance up I seeing Mr. H mansion far up on the hill—it come like "N" on a compass. Joan must be inside, with she friends, nibbling pastry. I don't want what is hers. Only what he promise me.

As we reaching closer and closer to the Junction, my heart start beating faster and faster. I rehearsing in my head everything I want to tell Mr. H. Muscles clenching everywhere—my hands, between my legs, my jaw. I get out the car in front Textile Kingdom and stare at the sign for a second. I did stand up right here last year—for the job interview—and I did feel the same way, like all my hope hanging on this one conversation.

A deep breath, then I push the door. Timing perfect: the store busy enough that the sales-girls all distracted, jostling one another for commission. I slip-in, between the bolts of cloth, and head down to the back of the store.

The office have a huge window, one-way glass. Mr. H could look out but people in the store can't see in. I wonder if he seeing me now. I know he in there: I smelling his Hong Wing coffee. I sure he have the newspaper spread open on the desk.

I reach the office door. It have a glass panel with some plastic mini-blinds. The rule is: if the blinds open, you just knock and walk in; if they close, you knock and wait.

The blinds close this morning. But through the crooked, curl-up strips I getting a side-view of Mr. H potbelly and the top of some woman head. I seeing enough to know that I shouldn't walk in. That I should spin 'round right now and leave the cloth-store quick, quick. But only one thought pounding in my head, heavy, heavy like a bass-line: *Is my fault, is my fault. I wait too long to come.*

Panic, all over my body, making me feel hot like when I did have dengue. I wring the doorknob and burst in the room. They hear, so they start scrambling. The girl ducking under the desk, Mr. H trying to fix his crotch. Then he spin his chair all the way 'round and, finally, he see me.

"Gail," he say, face ripening like a mango. He tapping under the desk. "You can go now, Sandy." She crawl out the room like a stinking cockroach.

"Is only a week," I say. "What you doing?"

"Well . . . I . . ." Mr. H start to say something in a shaky voice, then he stop.

We staring down one another. Inside, I telling myself to focus, begging myself not to get side-track by what I just see, reminding myself that I come with a higher purpose.

Then, is like Mr. H get over the shock of me appearing in his office. His tone change, getting rougher. "So why *are* you here, Gail? I hope to tell me you've come to your senses?"

"Yes," I say, pressing my thumbnails-and-them deep down in my finger-flesh. *Just say it, Gail. Just say it.*

"Well?" Mr. H ask.

I swallow the gallon of spit in my throat. "You don't have to leave Joan."

"What?"

"I was wrong to pressure you. I know your situation. I sorry."

Mr. H nodding, giving me a li'l half-smile. "Apology accepted. Now let's move on, shall we?" He showing me the chair on the other side of his desk.

I sit, feeling a li'l more at ease. "That's what I come to tell you. You does treat me good and I grateful. I ready for us to move on. Nothing really have to change. I not going and ask for more. Only thing: I was hoping we could get a bigger place now—with the baby coming, nah."

He blinking plenty. Now Mr. H talking slow, slow, like English ain't my mudder-tongue too. "Gail, have you made arrangements with the doctor?"

"No, I thought . . ."

"Why can't you get it?" He spring up, slamming he two fist on the desk. "I don't want any fucking child!" Like a bad pit-bull breaking the chain, Mr. H rush 'round the desk and coming at me. He grab my arm so hard I feel every one of his fingertips. He talking with his teeth lock-up like a gate. "What I want, Gail, is for you to stop dreaming. I want you to get your ass up, get out of my office and go call the fucking doctor. Now!"

He pulling me out the chair. Pulling hard.

"No," I say, trying to free-up my arm. "I not going nowhere!" I try to make myself heavy. I grip-on the handle but Mr. H so strong he make one pull and the aluminum chair spinning in a half-circle. "No! No!" Another big tug and I land on the tile floor. Damn hard: my insides shaking-up; I picturing purple jello. "Oh God, the child!" I say.

I try to scramble to my feet. My arm slipping from him, so Mr. H grab my ponytail. I crying and kicking, still screaming "No! No!" but he dragging me to the office door.

He screaming too, "Security! Security!" Footsteps running-up behind us. Two man grab me—one each side—and they pull me up. "No! No!" I refuse to walk so they carrying me through the store. My legs dragging on the ground like a invalid. Everybody watching—customers, sales-girls—everybody. The fuckers dump me outside on the pavement, in Pleasantview Junction, like a bag of stinking garbage. I cry out one long, last, "No!" and I pelt my shoes behind them.

As the taxi reach the apartment, I practically run out and kick-down my own front door. It still swinging on the hinges when I charge through the front-room and head straight for the chest-of-drawers—the one thing Janice ever give me. I remembering her advice now and yes, I know what side my bread butter on. I not bringing no innocent child into this world—this ketch ass world—call Pleasantview. I not watering down milk and rationing pampers—have the child crawling 'round with shit in he batty for half day—'cause I don't know when next I could buy. No sick child—snatty-nose turning pneumonia—deading on my hand 'cause I can't pay for doctor and medicine. Nah! Before it come to that, let me just done everything right now! Put everybody outta they damn misery!

I start groping inside the panty-drawer. My fingers knocking camphor-balls—*Clax! Clax!*– against the wood. Tiptoeing, I reach deeper and feel the box with the garnet ring. Then, I feel a long lump near the top right corner. That's it! I pull out the white envelope, rip the side open and the notepaper fly out, sailing down to the floor like a parachute. When I bend for it, all the cash in the envelope tumble out and settle 'round my foot—a money puddle. I step out of it and grab the cordless phone from next to the bed. I dial, but my fingers trembling so much, I have to start over. I make the appointment with Dr. Narayansingh—Tuesday at 10:00.

I make another call right afterward. To Mr. H cell phone. Vishnu answer, "Nah. The Bossman busy." He hang up.

I curl up on the bed, cordless in hand. I call back a million times but no answer. I just want this whole thing to be over. None of this woulda happen if I didn't get pregnant. I just want to go back to normal, like how it was before last week—before the baby—when I was the person Mr. H love, instead of the person he hate. But as I pull the coverlet over my head I have this sinking feeling: things might never be normal between me and Mr. H again. Not even if I go Tuesday. Is like something slip outta balance between us today. It have me asking myself if

I could ever lie-down under the man again, now that I know he ain't ever going to give me the price I calling. For what he taking. For what he did take that first day, in the office.

Is the feeling that I peeing-down myself that wake me. My eyes open to a room full-up with shadows—I must be sleep through the whole afternoon. I swipe inside my thigh. Wet. Sitting up, I stare at my fingers. A black water, black like Coca-Cola, but more thick. I smush it and it thin out enough for me to see it actually red—a dark, Beaujolais red. Blood. And something more spongy. Clots? Flesh? I feel another big gush pass from me. I jump off the bed and run to the back door screaming for Miss Ivy.

She find me on the floor, clutching my ball-up cotton dress like it could ever plug this leak.

"Father! Tell me you didn't try for yourself," she say, grabbing a kitchen towel.

"No," I say, "I was sleeping when . . . the blood . . . it just come down. . . ."

"Don't worry," she say, "sometimes they could still save it."

She bawling for Mr. Winston—he have a car—and they help me in the back-seat. By the time I rest my head on Miss Ivy lap, the towel between my legs soak-up and it have blood everywhere: on the upholstery, the glass, Miss Ivy robe; on Mr. Winston hands as he easing the vehicle out the long, narrow yard. My blood? The baby blood? It have any difference? Our blood. We losing too much.

I start screaming, over and over again, "Allyuh hurry up!

Please! Please!" because I suddenly realize this is my last chance. It have a baby—a real, live baby—right now in my belly. The two of we is a family right now, and we didn't have to ask nobody permission for that. And I realize that I never, ever in my life want anything more than what I want right now: to not lose this child, this chance. Every other fear done leak out and gone with all them clots.

Finally, the back tires drop from the yard to the road. Mr. Winston hands shaking as much as mines, but he bawling, "Don't worry, don't worry. My sister does work Casualty. I know the nurses-and-them. Don't worry."

"No! Not the General Hospital," I say. "Santa Marta Private. It closer. I have money. Reverse-back, reverse-back! Now!"

I squeeze Miss Ivy hand. Finally, I know the answer for what she did ask me last week. *Decide your mind,* she did say. *Who you really want,* she did say. So I tell her now, "The child, Miss Ivy, is only the child I want. Run quick. In the drawer by my bed: a white envelope."

The Ides of March

CORPORAL SHARPE

THE DOORS OF THE PLEASANTVIEW POLICE station had been locked since 11:00 PM. Anyone needing assistance would have to shout from the gate. Corporal Sharpe and his officers were snuggled away, upstairs, in the dormitory.

Sharpe lay with one arm behind his head, staring at the TV, twirling his moustache. He paid no attention to the movie, *Legends of The Fall*, or the officers' ole-talk. His mind was on the Station Diary's notes from the night before, the fifteenth of March:

> *Pleasantview Savannah . . . political rally of the PNM . . . police officers from Pleasantview Station as well as Northeastern Division Task Force (NEDTF) . . . PNM candidate, Mr. H, mounted the platform . . . gunshots . . . Mr. H unharmed . . . escorted to his vehicle . . . another loud explosion . . . NEDTF rushed to Mr. H's vehicle . . . Mr. H found bleeding . . . wound to his abdomen . . . female suspect and pistol seized by NEDTF and taken to another police station . . . Mr. H in critical condition. Enquiries continuing.*

The incident read like a highly organized, multi-person attack, the first shots within the venue being a diversion to get Mr. H to his car for the real shooter. A murder conspiracy. And the whole thing was big, big news too, except the newspapers had gotten an important detail wrong: it was NEDTF—those big-boys in Port of Spain—not the local Pleasantview police who had the suspect. This station's holding cell was empty. But still, Sharpe lamented, *if only* he'd been on duty last night! If *he* had been on duty, some of that favourable press might've rubbed off on him. In fact, if he had been on duty, he would have used every trick in the book to make himself a big fuckin' hero in the story. He needed that, he needed to change his image with The Seniors up in Police Headquarters. The new, holier-than-thou Commissioner was on a crusade against "bribe-taking officers". Allegedly, Sharpe's name had been called; allegedly a transfer—to some bushy station behind God's back—was coming by way of punishment. No way. Sharpe needed to stay right here in Pleasantview: his income depended on it.

Commercial break. Sharpe rose to pee and grab a snack. He shuffled his slippers across the black-and-white square tiles, and pictured a draughts board. The game was his favourite rumshop recreation and he felt its rules offered a tactical approach to life's problems. Rule 1: assess the board for weaknesses. In police-work, for sure, weaknesses were everywhere. Some informer not questioned, some evidence overlooked, some move not made—Sharpe just needed to find it. There had to be a way to huff this nice, fresh, shooting incident, to pocket it for his own benefit.

A noise came from outside. A metallic clanking: some-body banging the padlock against the gate. The sound alternated with that female ghetto-yodel Sharpe often heard around Pleasantview, "Oy-yo-yoiii! Oy-yo-yoiii! Officer! Officer!"

Thinking it was some drunkard whore wanting to sleep things off in the cell, Sharpe yawned and scratched his balls, ordering, "Sentry! See what going on there."

A young-police went to the metal louvres, always slanted so the lounging officers could look down upon the world without being seen themselves.

"Ahhm . . . Corpy," the young-police said, breath snagging, "it looking like . . . a bear?"

"A what?" Every officer, including Sharpe, rushed to the window.

Was it an after-effect of the movie, a trick of the mind? Sharpe had to blink a few times. In the dark, hobbling along the fence-line, there appeared to be a grizzly bear.

Sputtering overhead light showed the thing covered, head to foot, in dark fur. It bent over, grabbed something, then turned and hurled it toward the dormitory window. At the *plax!* of stone hitting louvre, everyone jumped back and Sharpe said, "Shiiittt!" but, in the same moment, he recognized it was not a bear but a human. And he recognized the human as Miss Ivy, that old lady from Panco Lane who paraded around in a fur coat.

Relief brought the baritone back to Sharpe's voice. "Goodnight, Tanty. What's your problem this hour?"

"Goodnight son," Miss Ivy replied, "the officer-in-charge, please."

"We closed, Tanty."

"Yeah, but it urgent. I have some hot, hot information."

"'Bout what, Tanty?" Sharpe was only asking for the

amusement of his men. He knew from his wife that Miss Ivy was a babysitter by day and a seer-woman by evening. Her area of specialty was cutting cards: using a deck of playing cards to foretell people's futures. She had quite a following—mostly women—and a kind of fearful reverence surrounded the old quenk. Nobody in Pleasantview messed with Miss Ivy because they believed she *knew* things. Sharpe didn't subscribe to that foolishness, though. He was sure she was here to waste police time with some nancy story, some imagined tragedy.

Then Miss Ivy said, "Is about the shooting last night. Mr. H, nah."

All eyes in the dormitory landed on Corporal Sharpe. He frowned and pursed his lips, assessing the board for his next move. He knew, like everybody else in Pleasantview, that Miss Ivy had worked as housekeeper in Mr. H's house for ages. The fur coat was a hand-me-down from Mrs. H, given to Miss Ivy upon retirement. Miss Ivy sashayed through the streets of Pleasantview wearing it, Sharpe believed, as a reminder to all that she was a woman with connections. It was possible, she might actually know something about this shooting. Something *he* should know as well.

"Ok, Tanty. I coming," he answered, and sent the young-police downstairs to open the gate and the door.

While he put on his uniform, Sharpe once more weighed his position and the stakes. Transfer *him* to some cane-land outpost? An officer like *him*, with fifteen years' experience? He could not suffer that indignity! Worse yet, if he was transferred, he'd have none of the leverage he enjoyed in Pleasantview. He would be starting over, and reduced to mere salary. How was he supposed to send his daughter to university on a policeman's salary? She'd been accepted to study medicine, starting this September. He had promised her that she could go.

The charge-room usually smelled of piss and mold, but this time, as Sharpe entered, he got the unmistakable odor of wet fur—a doggy smell. Miss Ivy's elbows and breasts sat on the counter as she scoured her face with a small red towel. When she saw him, she swung it onto her shoulder and began babbling.

"This thing on my mind whole day, Officer. Since it happen last night, I studying what to do. But I make up my mind. I don't have long again in this world—the Bible say three score and ten, and I is done three score and eight. I want to meet my maker with a clear conscience. So that's why I come. I have to say something."

Miss Ivy pounded the counter to the beat of the last words, then fell silent. She wanted Sharpe to draw it out of her, it seemed.

The Corporal leaned in, propping a hand under his chin. He affected the polite-but-bored expression of a bartender. Inside, though, he was feverish.

An excruciating moment passed before Miss Ivy blurted out, "I know who try to kill Mr. H."

"Us too, Tanty," Sharpe said, throat tight with this big lie.

"No, no. Allyuh *think* allyuh know. But allyuh only holding the trigger-puller. I know who is The Mr. Big behind the whole thing."

Sharpe's fingers climbed his chin to his moustache and

began twirling again. "Well," he said with a shrug. "I'm waiting. Give me a name."

"Nah, I have to start from the beginning. Allyuh have coffee? Bring some, nah? A chair too. And something to write."

MISS IVY

Exactly seven days before the PNM rally, seven days before Mr. H was shot, Miss Ivy had gotten a mysterious message from her best friend, Agnita: "Come this evening. It urgent. Walk with the cards."

But Miss Ivy wasn't sure she'd be able to make the visit. All the parents knew they were supposed to collect their children by five-thirty. Yet somebody always had an emergency. That day, March 8th , it had been five-year-old Jabari's mother. She'd sent a message with another parent to say she'd pick him up by seven. What could Miss Ivy do? She couldn't put the child out in the road. And, without any pickney of her own, Miss Ivy felt like a mother to them all.

Glancing off and on at the big Coca-Cola clock on the wall—the one with the polar bears, a Christmas gift from a parent—Miss Ivy chatted with Jabari as she fixed his dinner. She chopped the brown ends off his bread-and-butter sandwich, she added a second dollop of condensed milk to his tea—he liked it really sweet. The boy was standing on a cushion, pretending to surf, and though his eyes were fixed on Miss Ivy's black-and-white TV, his mouth chattered constantly.

"Mama Ivy, you know what?"

"What, son?"

"My Aunty have a new Hindu man name Jagroop."

Miss Ivy wanted to burst out laughing, but she was afraid Jabari would be spooked into silence. She played it cool, asking in a casual tone, "Eh-heh? How you know that?"

"He does come by we. He did bring a yellow UNC jersey for Aunty, but my Grandpa say she can't wear that and still live in we house."

Now Miss Ivy did burst out laughing. Jabari poor thing, he didn't know better. Election time was the worst time to leak out family politics. It could mean cut-eye from strangers, cold-shoulder from friends, or even "loss work" for his parents. But, as a seer-woman, Miss Ivy followed a personal code. "All skelingtons safe in my closet," she told her clients.

"I know your Grandpa since we small as you," she nodded at Jabari. "That sound just like him. A staunch PNM."

As he slurped his tea, Jabari prattled on about Jagroop: that he had a big black truck with shiny wheels, that he took the boy for drives in it, that they went all over the place, but they couldn't go to East Pleasantview because that's where Jagroop's family lived and he didn't want nobody to see.

Miss Ivy was still paying close attention when the boy's mother came hustling in, full of apologies. The polar bears on the wall said it was 6:25. Barely enough time to make it to Agnita's and back before dark, but Miss Ivy would try, for her best friend's sake.

Long, winding and dismal by day, Evans Street was downright scary as night approached. There were no proper street lamps. Some, long ago smashed by young fellas wanting privacy to do their business underneath. Others told their age with a constant hum and flicker. Things were even more dangerous these days, with the rash of election-time road works.

A fat wind came off the mountain and barged its way down the street, nearly tumbling Miss Ivy into an open manhole in the pavement. She caught her balance just in time, drew the fur coat even closer around her bulk, and began to cuss—not even caring if people in the passing cars noticed she was talking to herself.

"Suppose I did fall in and dead? Eh? Every election is the same damn thing! Suddenly, box-drain and pavement. Drain and pavement. As if we could eat and drink concrete. The people want water!"

"And light," Miss Ivy added, glancing up at the flickering street-lamps. What they really needed in Pleasantview was light.

Her hands stroked the puffy edge of the coat's hood as she consoled herself. Her old boss, Mr. H, would surely win the next election and, when he did, he would fix everything. He might have a lot of bad ways, he might be the village ram, fucking anything in sight, but you couldn't fault Mr. H for being a successful man-of-business: *he* would fix Pleasantview. Nobody could bully and get things done like him. Most people in Pleasantview were afraid of him but Miss Ivy wasn't. She and Mr. H, they had an understanding. To this day, every time she popped into his cloth-store, he'd always find her in the aisles, fold a couple hundreds into her palm and wink. Unofficial payment. For all the secrets she'd kept over the years, and for continuing to keep them now, especially from Mrs. H.

Agnita's bungalow came into view around the corner. Miss

Ivy could just make out her friend, seated on the tiny verandah of the house that had remained unchanged since they were children.

"Oyyyyy!" Miss Ivy hollered, as she swung the gate.

"Ayyyyy, girl!" Agnita replied.

Squeezing herself into the other wicker chair, Miss Ivy said, "So I see we get pavement, doux-doux."

"Yes, darling. Voting-time. That's why I ask you to come. This election go be trouble. I frighten bad." With the help of her cane and the chair handle, Agnita rose from the seat, even as she lowered her voice. "Come, let we go inside. Somebody might hear from the road."

"Is about my Hezekiah." Agnita's voice was somber at the dining table now. "I overhear him last night, he and he friends, in the bedroom."

"Who?" Miss Ivy asked. "Oh yes, your grandson. I so accustom calling the child 'Silence' like everybody else, I does forget he have a real name, yes. W'happen to he?"

"He get a work with Mr. H new campaign manager. You know who that is, right?"

Miss Ivy shook her head.

"You know him, man! A Indian fella. He own the fruits-place up in the Junction: Plenty Horn or Horn Plenty or something so. He used to be a big UNC man till couple weeks ago. I hear he was even going up for election against Mr. H. But he get catch in some whorehouse scandal, so UNC pull him off the slate. Jagroop, he name."

Miss Ivy's mind flipped back to little Jabari's story.

"Anyway," Agnita continued, "Jagroop switch sides. He turn PNM now. And Silence and them boys been working with him in Mr. H campaign office. At first I was glad; I say Silence might meet somebody to fix him up with a good, steady work. Instead of just liming with them fellas, thiefing fruits and selling them by the traffic lights. But you know what Jagroop, that stink mudder-so-and-so, ask my quiet, gentle grandson to do?"

"What, girl?" Miss Ivy asked, leaning so far forward the front legs of her chair began to complain.

"Jagroop pick up the boys yesterday and carry them for a long ride in he fancy truck—like he did want privacy, nah. He say: since UNC shame he and he family, they must lose this election. He say he have a plan, and . . ."

Agnita began to sniffle and shake her head, as if she couldn't bear to explain further.

While she waited, Miss Ivy clucked her tongue, offered Agnita napkins from the plastic holder on the table, and wondered if her friend knew the talk on the street about Silence: that he wasn't such a quiet, gentle boy anymore; that he sold something other than fruits now; that he'd recently become a foot-soldier for Lost Boyz gang. Or was Agnita just like all the other Pleasantview mothers and grandmothers? Playing deaf and dumb until they ended up on the news crying, "He was a good boy, you know!"

Agnita continued in a shaky voice, "The big PNM meeting is next week—the fifteenth. Jagroop paying them boys to shoot at the stage while Mr. H talking. Not to kill him, eh. Just to frighten everybody. Jagroop say it go look like is UNC put a hit on Mr. H and everybody go turn against UNC and vote PNM."

"Oh gaddoye!" Miss Ivy felt as if the short, kinky hairs at the base of her corn-rows just went dead straight. "What the ass this Jagroop-fella trying to do? Start a war? Suppose they miss and the bullet catch Mr. H?"

Miss Ivy had spent her entire sixty-eight years inhaling the rancid drain water of West Pleasantview. She'd lived through more elections and more funerals than most people in this overgrown scrap-yard of a town. But Miss Ivy couldn't recall, in all her years, a single instance of someone being shot for political reasons.

"That is why I ask you to walk with your cards and everything," Agnita said. "I so worried 'bout Silence!" She began wailing.

Miss Ivy wasted no time. She dug into her purse for the cards and began a long, vigorous shuffling. Her upper lip perspired and the deep furrows of her forehead slipped down to become a visor over her eyes. Silently, she begged God to grant her the gift—just this once—to really see the future. This wasn't some domestic, who-fuckin'-who bacchanal, her usual fortune-telling domain. This was serious. This could be life or death. For either Mr. H or Agnita's grandson.

"You have anything belonging to Silence? Something personal," Miss Ivy asked.

Agnita, veteran of these rituals, was ready. "Look," she replied, "I take this from the drawer. It clean." From the pocket of her house-dress came a pair of jockey-shorts. Eggplant in color, with white piping.

Miss Ivy sprinkled the underwear with holy water from a tiny bottle. Then, gripping the crotch, she closed her eyes and began a rolling chant, "O Mother, O Mother! Mother Sita. O Mother! Mother Mary. O Mother! Mother Earth. O Mother!"

She opened her eyes and grabbed up the deck. Agnita gasped.

Miss Ivy began flipping cards expertly, making a snapping noise as each left the pack. At the first King, she stopped, studied the card and nodded.

Pleasantview people loved face-cards. Yes, she'd milk the face-cards for Agnita.

She flipped again until . . . a Queen. Then, another King.

Miss Ivy had enough for a story. She slammed the pack down. "That's it! The Queen of Hearts—a woman—will come between the King of Diamonds and the King of Spades. The first King is Mr. H—the money-man. Then, you see how a Spade shape like a upside-down heart? That second King is Jagroop—deceitful. But don't worry, Silence ain't showing up nowhere in these cards. He safe. Like Jesus briefcase."

CORPORAL SHARPE

Corporal Sharpe raised his palm to silence Miss Ivy. All this shit about cutting cards! Was she playing a game, leading him on? She was talking too fast and acting too cocky. He needed to put her in check.

"Tanty, wait, wait, wait . . ."

"Officer, I swear to God! Jagroop send Silence to shoot Mr. H."

"Maybe," Sharpe said, "but I have questions. Answer honest and I might believe this whole nancy story you come with. But lie, and I will kick you out this station *tout suit*, you hear?"

"Ask me, ask me. Anything."

Sharpe looked Miss Ivy in the eyes and deployed an old-police tactic. He asked a question for which he already had the answer. "You does really see the future in them cards? Or you is a con-woman? The truth, eh."

Miss Ivy's chest heaved, then she slumped into the chair, arms falling from the desk in a surrendering way. She stared at the ceiling, and answered in almost a whisper.

"I ain't no con-woman, officer. Is not as black-and-white as that."

In truth, she *did* know things, she said. But not because she saw them in the cards. She knew because the rumor-mill in Pleasantview was that good, because she was older and wiser than most, and because the best peddlers of gossip were the children she babysat every day. She wasn't a con-woman, she insisted, because she'd never charged for her services. Those who could afford left a little tip, but the money really didn't matter. "I just want to help, to lend a li'l guidance," she said, "and I know Pleasantview people does only take advice if it wearing supernatural clothes."

"So you was bold-face lying to Miss Agnita? Your so-called best friend?"

Miss Ivy met Sharpe's eyes, but with a glint in her own.

"Officer, come nah, man. You woulda do any different? *You?*"

Sharpe studied the old lady, tapping the ballpoint pen against his nose. He'd lied plenty times to save his daughter's, his wife's feelings. *Yes, we could afford med school. Yes, you could start in September. No, I never sleep with that woman.* Lying was sometimes the right move when dealing with people you love.

"Fine," Sharpe conceded. "But suppose you lying to me now?"

"The man confess, Officer. To my face, Jagroop admit everything."

Corporal Sharpe grew itchy inside his uniform. Jagroop was one of his best-paying Pleasantview businessmen—never late with "taxes". Every week, Sharpe visited The Horn of Plenty and filled a basket with fruit and vegetables. Like any other customer, he rested the basket near the cashier, Jagroop's son. The produce was bagged and returned, but always without the Corporal having paid, and always with something extra in one of the bags—"a coil": a rubber-banded roll of hundred-dollar notes. That was how Jagroop got such zealous police response to shoplifters, and to street vendors trying to claim the pavement outside his store. That was why Jagroop's customers never got towed from the no-parking zone.

Yes, Jagroop paid well, but sometimes a man must sacrifice a pawn here, to earn a crown there. If Sharpe was going to serve up Jagroop to The Seniors, he needed more conclusive evidence from Miss Ivy.

For the first time since the old lady began speaking, Sharpe opened his notebook and uncapped his pen. "Gimme it," he said. "Gimme every last word."

MISS IVY

The weather-lady had said that sunrise on March 9th , the day after Miss Ivy's chat with Agnita, would be at 5:45 a.m. Miss Ivy pressed her fists deeper into the pockets of her fur coat and leaned against the wall, admiring the sky's transition from black to the crisp blue of a new day. How, she wondered, could that weather-lady know the exact time God was going to hang up the sun? How? Miss Ivy shook her head in awe. What she wouldn't give to be able to do that, to know the mind of God.

As the grey blanket fell from Pleasantview, Miss Ivy moved to the lamp post across the street from Jagroop's house.

After what Agnita had told her yesterday, she had to see for herself. This "Jagroop": did he look like the kind of man who'd be as reckless as Agnita described? Miss Ivy could usually spot a son-of-a-bitch if she paid attention. Facial expressions, mannerisms, a kind of impatience in the way they dealt with small things—these signs predicted fuckery in bigger things. She needed to observe Jagroop in his own yard, in the honesty of his private world, before he stepped onto the stage of his shop.

The two-story concrete house was in East Pleasantview— just as Jabari had said. A cluster of colorful religious flags— jhandis—in the corner, further confirmed Jabari's story: the man was Hindu. And, one of the vehicles parked on the property was a big, black truck—just like Jabari had described.

Miss Ivy watched Jagroop emerge into the fenced front yard. He wore full white: a V-neck T-shirt that barely covered his belly and a traditional dhoti below. On his feet were leather slippers. He puttered around. Sometimes she saw him clearly, other times she lost him behind the concrete posts of the wall. She heard the gush of water from a tap a few times; the clang of a bell a few times. Once or twice, her nose picked up the sweetness of incense. Jagroop was doing his morning devotions.

Miss Ivy wondered what he was praying for, the deceitful bastard.

Then she felt guilty for the thought. The man was praying. What if Agnita was mistaken about him? Even if Agnita was right, at least Jagroop was a praying man. There was a chance then: to appeal to his conscience, to stop the shooting. She could say she was a seer-woman, that the cards had sent her to warn him. He was Hindu, they believed in animal gods. It wouldn't be a stretch to make him believe in the god of the cards.

Jagroop sauntered back into view. He picked up a hose and began spraying two piles of dog shit.

Miss Ivy crossed the road.

"Morning, Mr. Jagroop," she called with more confidence than she felt. "A minute, please."

Jagroop's head whipped around. He frowned, then his eyes fell to her coat. "Wait," he said, "you's that babysitter from over-so?" He pointed west. "We don't need nobody again, you know. My daughter and she baby done gone back New York."

"No, Mr. Jagroop. Is not that. I come 'bout something else."

Jagroop stopped squeezing the nozzle and walked toward Miss Ivy. The dragging hose gave him a dragon look that made her pores raise and turn bumpy.

She pressed on. "I know you working for Mr. H now. I used to work for him too. And it so happen, I know people working in your campaign office too. Like Hezekiah Watkins. He is a good boy, you know, Mr. Jagroop. The only help to his grandmother."

Still Jagroop said nothing. He began watering the petunias along the walkway to his gate.

Miss Ivy talked louder, faster. She needed to capture his attention, to lure him closer, so she could reason with him.

"I's cut cards, you know, Mr. Jagroop. That's what I come to tell you. The cards talking. They saying things 'bout the PNM rally next week. Bad things."

Jagroop came to the gate. They were now face to face, only the curvy metal in between. Miss Ivy got a blast of minty toothpaste as Jagroop said, "Bad things like what?"

It was the snarl: the glossy gold tooth, the flaring nostrils while his eyes narrowed to bullet points. That, and the mocking manner: how he threw his shoulders back and thrust out his chest, as if to dare her. Jagroop's reaction stuck in Miss Ivy's craw, convincing her that he was indeed a dangerous man. Dangerous to Mr. H, dangerous to Pleasantview.

"Listen, Mister Gentleman!" she said. "I go make it my business to be at that rally. I coming early to plant my bench near the police-and-them. And if anything happen . . . if I so much as hear a juice box explode, I going straight to the corporal-in-charge and tell him everything I know 'bout you."

"Woman . . ."

"And furthermore, after I finish by the police, I coming here by your sweet wife to tell she 'bout you and your nigger-woman, and the nastiness you does have that young lady doing inside that black truck."

"Look, haul your mudder-cunt! Now! Before I let go the

dog. Move!" At the last word, Jagroop aimed the nozzle at Miss Ivy and pulled the trigger.

Cold water stung her face, invaded her nose, filled her mouth, and almost took out her eye. She doubled over. She bawled for Jesus. But Jagroop was merciless. Miss Ivy fell backwards from the gate, into the open box-drain where he left her, covered in wet fur.

CORPORAL SHARPE

Corporal Sharpe's mind seemed to have grown six legs and was now skittering around, between his ears. If Miss Ivy's account was true, then Jagroop hadn't actually confessed to anything, but he *had* acted very guilty. No doubt, he was involved in the shooting.

Miss Ivy was in the toilet—had been for some time—and while he waited, Sharpe re-read his notes, comparing all he'd heard to what he'd read in the Station Diary: *female suspect and pistol seized*. Yet, the only female Miss Ivy had mentioned was old Agnita.

By the time the bathroom door slammed, Sharpe had decided on his final move.

"Bonjay-O!" Miss Ivy said, announcing her return. "This shooting thing had me cork-up since last night, Officer. Nerves, nah." She plopped into the chair and let out a big sigh. "So what now?" she asked, drumming the desk with fingers resembling ginger root.

Sharpe glared at the old lady until she began to fidget with his pencil-caddy.

Then, he slammed his palm unto the desk, making her startle. "Alright, Tanty," he said. "*Your* confession now. You knew what Jagroop was planning. And you did nothing? You didn't tell nobody? Allyuh woman love to talk. If you didn't want the man dead, you woulda tell somebody. I feel you holding out on me. You protecting somebody. I want to know who. Who did you tell and who else is involved? And remember: one lie, and you lock-up for wasting police time."

MISS IVY

The day after Miss Ivy's visit to Jagroop, she buzzed at the double-gates of Elysium, the Santa Marta mansion of Mr. H. She'd wanted to get there earlier, to be alone with Mrs. H, but she'd struggled to find a taxi willing to come up the mountain on this rainy day. Miss Ivy arrived feeling hurried, unsettled for the task she'd set herself.

The weekly fortune-telling-tea-party had just begun, yet the ladies were already onto their second bottle of wine. They were already giggly, behaving like teenagers. Some sat with bare feet tucked under, others draped themselves across patio chairs. With their lightish skin, teased hair and black-rimmed eyes, they looked to Miss Ivy like a harem of old-ass Cleopatras. Wine glasses swirling, they cheered for Miss Ivy when she appeared in the doorway between the kitchen and patio.

There was a loud creak as Mrs. H shut the oven and said, "Ivy, darling, I thought you'd forgotten us."

Miss Ivy spun around. "No, no, Mrs. You know Ivy would never do that. Once Ivy say she comin', bet your bottom dollar she comin'. I ready to start. Come, nah?" she said, talking too fast, babbling like the children she babysat.

Mrs. H answered, "Go ahead, I'll just be a minute," while she fussed with oven knobs.

Miss Ivy hurried into Mr. H's den, where she conducted her sessions. It was the perfect setting: heavy drapes, dark wood and the amber shadows from an antique lamp. Today, though, Miss Ivy's hands shook as she set up the cards she'd prepped and practiced with last night.

The plan was simple: convince Mrs. H her husband was in mortal danger and that, according to the cards, March fifteenth was an unlucky date for him to appear in public. Wasn't that the truth? So why was she so nervous? She stared at the door, crushing the empty card box while she waited for Mrs. H. Would the cards stick? Would she drop the pack and throw everything out of sequence? In all her years of "seeing", Miss Ivy had never before worried about these things. She'd always been confident, but now she felt her palms growing more and more clammy with every passing second—as if she was balling toolum, molasses candy.

Confidence was King, she reminded herself. A long time ago, she used to wonder why Mrs. H collected paintings and sculptures of black people all over the house. It took about a decade, but then Miss Ivy figured it out: Mrs. H felt black people were mystical in some way. Closer to God or something. Just put on a colorful head-tie and talk mumbo-jumbo with confidence and Mrs. H bought in. Yes, confidence was King.

Like that time when their daughter, Kimberley, was little and had spied Mr. H trying to bend Miss Ivy over the kitchen sink. She had radiated only confidence when she swore on her ancestors' graves that she'd been choking on a chennette seed, and that Mr. H had been saving her life. Mrs. H had believed.

And all the other times, when Mrs. H had gotten whiff of Mr. H's womanizing. Miss Ivy would always listen with a flat, blank face and then work the cards to comfort the woman. Miss Ivy felt responsible not only to keep house, but also the family's secrets and domestic peace. She didn't want to work for a divorced hag—Pleasantview people respected you more when you worked for a proper Santa Marta family.

Mrs. H entered into the room, took a tired breath, then wilted onto the tufted sofa where Miss Ivy sat. The leather made a farting noise, which sapped the power of the moment and eased the tension in Miss Ivy's nerves.

Mrs. H gave a hand flick, to signal she was ready.

First, the opening chant, then Miss Ivy picked up the cards. She flipped and flipped until the King of Clubs appeared. She turned the next card: as planned, it was the Two of Clubs.

"Humph!" she grunted.

Mrs. H gasped. "What? Tell me."

"You sure you want to know, Mrs.? It not too nice, nah."

"Oh for God's sake, Ivy! Why do you think you're here?"

"Well, is about The Mister."

"I knew it! That son-of-a-bitch is still screwing that girl who used to work in the store, not so? I heard a rumor that she's pregnant. It's true, isn't it? Tell me!" Mrs. H picked up a card and flung it in Miss Ivy's direction.

It was true. Miss Ivy knew the girl well. In fact, until recently, she and nineteen-year-old Gail Archibald had lived in the same yard in Panco Lane. She'd been Gail's confidante about the affair with Mr. H; and she'd been at the hospital that dread, dread night when Gail had lost the child. She'd eavesdropped as Gail kept calling Mr. H's phone, begging his driver to pass on the message. And she'd held Gail, letting her cry day after day, when Mr. H didn't show. Miss Ivy had been the one to call Gail's mother to say, "Come for your daughter. It look like this thing sending she mad." And it was Miss Ivy who'd helped pack up Gail's apartment.

Miss Ivy bent over now, retrieved the card from the floor, slowly, giving bitterness time to drain from her face.

"What the hell is it, Ivy! You're trying my patience."

"Ok, Mrs., let me explain. See how the King of Clubs ain't have no sharp edges? He is a peaceful ruler. That is Mr. H. And you know: King always count as thirteen. Now watch the next card: Two of Clubs. Same suit, so we add: thirteen and two is . . .?"

"Fifteen."

"Exactly. That number mean anything special to you or Mr. H? Could be somebody age? Or a date?"

Mrs. H stared into the river landscape hanging on the wall, her eyes darting like she was counting the bamboo. "Fifteen . . . fifteen?" she mused. "The only thing I can think of is the rally. But I don't know . . ."

"The PNM rally?"

"Yes, it's next Wednesday—the fifteenth. You're attending, right? It's his big moment. He'd want you there."

Miss Ivy tapped her temple, began swaying. "I getting a serious bad-vibes 'bout that date. Let we see if is because of the rally."

Counting aloud, Miss Ivy flipped fifteen more cards. "Ah!

You see? Ten. The most crowded card it have. And is Clubs too. That is the damn thing self! Mr. H need to stay away from all crowds on the fifteenth."

"But how can he do that, Ivy? We're in the middle of an election. The *Party* has set that date for the rally, they're desperate to win Pleasantview. He can't just disappear."

"I don't know Mrs., but the cards don't lie. And you see this Clubs on top of Clubs? Is too much black—it mean death. Mark my words, whatever bad breeze going to blow on the fifteenth, it bringing death with it."

"So what do I do?" Mrs. H grabbed Miss Ivy's wrist.

Miss Ivy looked down at the lady's see-through, blue-veined fingers, squeezed together, resembling a nest of wood-slave lizards. In the twenty years she'd worked there, Miss Ivy could count, on one hand, the number of times Mrs. H had ever touched her. Skin to skin. Santa Marta ladies only dirtied their hands like that when they were desperate.

Miss Ivy dropped the meek-and-mild act, looked her ex-boss straight in the eye, her tone losing all its flattery. "Fake sick. Fake injury. Beg him. Bully him. Make the children or the grandchildren bully him. Fuck him, if necessary. Do whatever you have to do. But keep your husband from that meeting."

CORPORAL SHARPE

"That is everything, Officer. The whole truth and nuttin' but the truth. I really tried to save the man. You don't find so?" Miss Ivy dragged the red towel from her shoulder and dabbed her eyes.

"Yes, you did. You real try." Sharpe said, anxious to get rid of the old lady now. He had a phone call to make. He got up, walked around to her side of the desk and palmed her shoulder as if his touch could heal. "Good work, Tanty. I'll take it from here."

Miss Ivy's body sagged—Sharpe felt it through his fingers—so he helped her up and proffered her fur coat.

Yet she wouldn't leave. Sharpe had to coax her to the door. And then to the gate. She kept stopping, asking questions—like she couldn't walk *and* talk. When were they going to pick up Jagroop? Would they go easier on Silence? Was there a witness protection program for her?

Sharpe told lie after lie. Finally, he locked the station gate and watched Miss Ivy hobble off into the night.

He felt sorry for her. Had she truly possessed the gift of sight, she would've grasped what Sharpe had come to understand while she spoke, she would've made smarter moves.

Back inside, he grabbed the station phone and called the NEDTF office in Port of Spain. He gave his name, rank, station and asked to speak to the senior officer on duty. He said he'd been asked by the family to enquire into the wellbeing of a detainee: one Gail Archibald. The officer replied that she was well and had begun eating, although she kept babbling some gibberish about a dead baby.

"She really do it?" Sharpe asked, "Just between us old-police, tell me, nah?"

"Yeah, Batch. She confess to everything. But don't worry: the bitch stark, raving mad. She go get-off."

Sharpe thanked the officer and hung up. No conspiracy. Gail had acted alone. But still, other shots had been fired on the night of the fifteenth. Sharpe would find Jagroop, unmask him, watch him panic and then offer to keep his dirty little secret. Provided, of course, the coils grew fatter from now on—fat as truck tires—and they would have to follow Sharpe, wherever on the island he was transferred.

Sharpe opened the buttons of his uniform shirt, and rocked back in the chair, staring at the ceiling. He heard no TV in the dormitory, no voices either; the officers were all asleep, he guessed. He lifted the phone again and called his house, knowing full well his daughter would be up studying at this hour. He just wanted to tease her, like he still did sometimes, and say, "Daddy love you, you know? Daddy love you bad, bad, bad."

Home

Kimberley didn't know that her estranged father, Mr. H, cloth magnate, up-and-coming politician, had been shot. While *he* was in Trinidad, sliding from the leather backseat to become a heap on the floor of his car, *she* was still in self-imposed exile in Barbados, her tongue travelling down the ripples of her "roommate" Rachel's sculpted stomach.

Kimberley's bedroom windows were open, letting in the groans of the Atlantic Ocean as it churned and twisted and crashed itself against the brown curves of the island's south coast. So easy to mistake the sound for Rachel's pulse, gushing as it climbed her trembling thighs. Kimberley held them up and open, knees in stiff peaks, knowing from experience that resistance heightened the intensity for Rachel. Soon, though, the ocean was drowned by another noise, the kind you might expect to hear at a murder, with Rachel bucking and shaking as if her very life was leaking away.

There would be a few minutes, Kimberley knew, of Rachel being deaf, dumb and blind. That crucial interlude, when Kimberley could satisfy *herself*. She'd become expert at doing it secretly, noiselessly, with nothing but a tiny lurch and an almost imperceptible gurgle. Rachel must never know—she would misunderstand, read too much into it. She was a Pilates instructor, not a lawyer; she didn't grasp fine distinctions the way Kimberley did. She hadn't done the research the way Kimberley had. She didn't know that a perfectly normal woman, like Kimberley, could experience physical arousal with another woman and not be psychologically aroused. Intent, *i.e. mens rea*, was everything—lawyers knew this; without it, a person was innocent.

Kimberley was innocent. She was not a lesbian.

She assured herself of this as she rolled her forehead across Rachel's belly, clutched the bedskirt and waited for her own heart rate to slow.

She had never been the instigator of these midnight trysts—it was always Rachel. And Kimberley only obliged because she wanted Rachel to be happy; they'd been through so much together. When Kimberley was in law school back home in Trinidad, Rachel had been the first to respond to her ad for a roommate. One look at this pretty, hazel-eyed foreign student with the sun-bleached dreadlocks and wooden necklaces, and Kimberley knew Rachel would not last long in accounting school. But she'd rented her the room anyway. And when Mr. H had thrown them out of the apartment and cut off Kimberley's allowance, it was Rachel who'd found a new place for them and paid the rent that whole year. And when law school was over, it was Rachel who'd said, "Why you don't come home with me to Barbados? We got law firms there too, you know." And it was Rachel who'd asked a favor and gotten Kimberley a job. This new breezy Barbados life, out of Mr. H's reach, was so different to her life in Trinidad. This was a life Kimberley had herself grafted, from only those things she could control. And she owed it all to Rachel.

So whenever, off-and-on, Rachel came reaching, putting Kimberley's hands where she wanted her to start, saying—no, almost chanting—"I need it, Kim," Kimberley found herself doing things she wouldn't for anyone else but Rachel.

But still, she was not a lesbian. Not at all. Neither of them was. They were Soulmates With Benefits.

Rachel's hands left Kimberley's short curls, gripped her arms, tugged. Tonight was about to end as these trysts always did, Kimberley expected: a cuddle, some whispered good-nights, then Rachel would slip from the bed, float away to her own room and, by next morning, it would be as if nothing had ever happened between them. Soulmates With Benefits.

Instead, Rachel mounted Kimberley and used perfect teeth to pluck at the thin strap of Kimberley's pajama-top.

"It's my turn, it's my turn," she sang, squeezing Kimberley's breast.

"No, that's okay," Kimberley said, trying, gently, to pry her off—as she'd done the few other times Rachel had ever tried to touch her in this way.

"Come nuh, lemme do it," Rachel whined, nibbling lower and lower.

"No, I . . ."

Rachel yanked the strap. Kimberley's breast rolled out sideways onto the sheet, like a dead thing. Rachel swooped down and swallowed the nipple.

"Stop it!" Kimberley's arms shot out, her skin prickly with a heat she knew well: shame. She'd felt it last week, too: standing naked before the doctor in Bridgetown because her insurance had demanded a physical.

Rachel fell backwards off the bed, her head sounding a dull thud on the floor.

Blunt force trauma. LAWYER KILLS LIVE-IN LOVER: Kimberley pictured the sordid headline as she scrambled up, trying to stuff herself back into the pajama, trying to extend a hand to Rachel, trying to apologize. Her body burned as if she'd been drinking Cockspur rum straight from the bottle all night.

Rachel slapped Kimberley's palm away and stood. "What the rasshole wrong with you, girl?" she asked, pushing Kimberley. Twice.

Kimberley let her, because a lawyer should be just and fair, because she had assaulted Rachel and a victim should be allowed to retaliate. So, from the edge of the mattress, where Rachel's last push had landed her, Kimberley stammered, "Sorry, sorry . . ."

"*Cheese d'on bread!*" Rachel exclaimed, in her rankest Bajan accent. "So you cyah try just once, Kim? You always gotta behave like somebody killin' you?" Rachel's chest heaved. She made fists, then abandoned them, splaying her fingers, clutching for something that wasn't there.

"Look, I over-reacted. Sorry. But it's your fault: you surprised me," Kimberley said.

Rachel had never, ever been this aggressive—not in bed, not in any aspect of their life together over the last three years. Sure, she was a free spirit in many ways—with her essential oils, pottery classes, and the ugly organic vegetables she grew on the balcony—but Rachel had always respected Kimberley's rules. Personal care items—especially toothbrushes—were not for sharing. Always knock before entering and ask before taking. And, most importantly, no means no.

"I don' understan' you," Rachel said, deflating, finally, onto the bed next to Kimberley. "You does keep nuff noise sayin' you love me, you love me, but you never want *me* to touch *you*. Wha' kinda love that is?" She bent and picked a pillow off the floor, hugged it tight. In the sunset glow of the bedside lamp, she looked so tortured.

It made Kimberley feel like a bad person.

"I do love you," she said, sliding closer, stroking Rachel's cheek. "But I told you before, babe, I'm just not comfortable with . . ."

"Exposure. Yeah, yeah. You like to use big words like that, and make every damn thing sound so highfalutin . . . when it really very simple."

"Look at *me*, then go watch in the mirror at *you*. See any difference?" Kimberley said.

"No, don't start that shyte, this hour," Rachel replied, shaking her head.

"Watch these hands . . . two slabs of pork, right?" Kimberley said. This kind of self-deprecation came easily to her. She hated her body, always had.

"Nuttin' wrong with your hands," Rachel said, rolling her eyes and fiddling with her silver toe ring.

"See, you can't understand, because you look like a model. I look like the box the shittin' stove came in." Kimberley's ugliness was *ipso facto* obvious, so she found it easy to talk about *that*, instead of the other reasons she didn't want Rachel to make love to her—those were harder to mention because she didn't fully understand them herself.

"Stop it, nuh!" Rachel begged, clamping her ears.

"Yup, like Mummy always says: I'm cursed. All Daddy's Syrian genes—I have them. Short, square, hairy, and just plain . . ." Kimberley let the sentence trail off and hung her head for dramatic effect, waiting for Rachel to retreat in a fluster of apologies.

But Rachel got up, pillow still in hand, and began pacing the isthmus of carpet between the bed and the closet. "That is bare, feckin' shyte!" she said. "Is all in your feckin' head. I try and I say: lemme show you, nuh, babes? But, no, watch we: I *still* cyah touch you when we in public, I *still* cyah touch you when we by weself. We just stuck. Is like one big, fleckin' experiment for you, Kim. Well, I tired. *Cor blimey*, is time this relationship get growin'!"

Kimberley shut her eyes and squeezed her temples—another habit she'd inherited from her father—reviewing all the anomalies of the last few months. Rachel had broken up with that last guy, Errol the Engineer, in January and things had been different since. Usually, within two weeks, she'd have another man on the scene, but she hadn't mentioned anyone this time. And she'd been more clingy than usual too: crawling into Kimberley's bed more often, asking "You love me?" all the time. Other questions too: Asking to accompany Kimberley to work functions ("No!"); trying to hold her hand on Broad Street ("Hell no!"); asking, "Where we goin' from here?" ("What the ass wrong with here?")

"You listening to me?" Rachel cried.

The pillow hit Kimberley's face, then fell to the floor.

Kimberley launched from the mattress to jab her finger into Rachel's face. "*I* treat *you* like an experiment? Don't talk shit, girl," she said, then turned on her heel and headed for the door. She was almost there when she found herself marching back to Rachel. "Listen, I know what going on here. Errol fuck-up your head and now you depressed and taking it out on me. But you's the one experimenting, Rachel. Since we land in Barbados is you who been hopping from dick to dick then running back to me to lick your wounds." She took two giant steps toward the door again, then two giant steps back. "I been right here all the time. I've never even touched anyone else. I don't ask you nothing, I don't police what you do with your pussy, because all I really want is your heart. So don't talk to me about experimenting. You's the queen of that!"

The fogginess in Rachel's eyes cleared and something more edgy took its place. She aimed her chin at Kimberley and said, "Awright then. I done experimentin'. Mummy and Daddy invite us to the beach house again. Saturday. We goin' this time."

"So you not *asking*, you *ordering* me to go?"

"Well, you need to come, Kim, because I tellin' them 'bout us. I mekkin' it official—since we shuttin' down the lab and done-ing the experiment, right?"

Kimberley wound her arm around the bed's tall wooden post, effectively tying herself in place. "Tell them what about us? What exactly?" she asked, in the cautioning voice she used with dishonest clients.

"Kim, them ain't stupid," Rachel snarled. "I sure they suspect already. We goin' start by tellin' them and, when you see we have their support, I know you goin' feel different 'bout—"

"About what?"

"You know . . . coming-out."

Kimberley's knees weakened; she leaned hard against the post, causing the bed to creak under her weight. These last few months, all the tiny cracks and chips in Rachel's usually predictable behavior—Kimberley saw a pattern glinting now. Everything came together to form a hideous, mocking mosaic.

"Rachel, dear," she breathed the words up from the depths of her patience, "coming-out is for *lesbians*."

They locked eyes, both listening, it seemed, to the L-word rebounding off the walls.

"Well, I tellin' them," Rachel cried. In that lamp-light, her shriveling brown face was a sapodilla spoiling in the sun.

And in that instant—it must've been a premonition—Kimberley thought of Mr. H. Him, standing over the gardener, making sure the sapodilla tree was planted exactly where she (eight-year-old "Kimmy") had wanted it in the backyard of their family home in Trinidad. And, years later, him kicking her out and calling her a "big, fat, nasty queer". For a long moment, Kimberley felt herself swept up and swirling in a kind of vertigo of hate, but she wasn't sure who she was hating. Mr. H? Or Rachel?

She released the bed and took a step toward Rachel, not knowing what to say or do, desperate to pick up the pillow, slam it into Rachel's face and hold it there until she recanted her stupid, stupid plan to expose their relationship. Rachel must've sensed it. She shouldered past Kimberley and ran from the bedroom, across the corridor, to her own.

Kimberley spent the next day, Friday, in a pissy mood, and it didn't help that the managing partner kept needling her about a legal opinion for a Hong Kong client. He wanted it by day's end.

Things got even worse when, around three o'clock, she said to her secretary, "No, you don't need another coffee break, Beatrice. I'm waiting on those pages," causing Beatrice to eye her from head to toe, wheel back the chair, grab her handbag and sashay out of the office saying, "I don' need dis ras, nuh," under her breath.

By five o'clock, Kimberley had two-finger-typed almost seven pages, and was exhausted. Flipping through the scribbles in her yellow legal pad, she estimated at least another forty-five minutes of work . . . on a Friday evening. If only she hadn't been so impatient and nit-picky with Beatrice all day! She dug her daily planner from the nest of papers and jotted a note for Monday: *Take B to lunch. Maybe buy flowers?*

Needing a break, she turned from the static glare of the screen to stare out the window at the Bridgetown sun: it always shone so fiercely at this hour, clung so desperately to the sky, fighting against its fate—its own nature—just before leaking like an injured egg yolk into the dark porcelain sea. Kimberley never noticed the sun in Trinidad, but now her eyes followed a length of light as it passed through the window bringing a million specks—the fine print of the Universe—to her attention. Rachel was wrong; life was complicated.

She returned to the computer screen, took a bite of the flying-fish cutter that had been sitting on her desk since lunchtime—the bread now dry and choking. She ate slowly, skimming the last paragraph she'd written: International Business Corporation . . . Hong Kong resident . . . Barbadian courts . . . separate legal personality . . . Blah, blah, blah. Her brain felt clogged with other, more personal arguments.

She could *not* be a lesbian. A lesbian was a woman who habitually engaged in sex with other women. Kimberley didn't have *sex*-sex with Rachel, and she didn't want to have sex with anybody at all. Not that she had anything against intercourse, per se. In fact, had she not met Rachel she would've done it by now, with some man. The moment she graduated, Mr. H would've found a suitable match for her with some other Syrian duckling—even if he had to import one from Syria itself. Like her older sister, Kimberley had grown up knowing she would have to marry for profit, for dynasty, and she and her husband would have sex for those same reasons.

But Rachel had changed all that. Their very first time together, Kimberley discovered a power that had freed her, but also frightened her. All the things she didn't know how to do, things she'd never done before, they soon came naturally as she embraced the delicious, illicit power of devouring another person. To tear at them with your teeth and hands, to pry them open, to spread them wide, to reach until the tip of your tongue discovers their softest core. To take that too: to curl your lips over it and swallow the last of their dignity. To leave them with nothing but their own plaintive cries. To own them.

Kimberley didn't want any human being to own her. Not even Rachel.

The thought made her skin itch. She began typing again, calling out the words, pounding them out on the keyboard and willing herself to concentrate on their meaning.

Her cellphone rang. *Oh shit*, Rachel.

Kimberley let it ring through a few cycles while she

steadied her vocal chords. When she did answer, and Rachel said, "He-e-y," in the lilting way that implied, "I'm sorry and ready to make up," Kimberley's pinched shoulders released.

Rachel knew what she'd done, how unreasonable she'd been.

"So, Pelican, right, babes? What time?" Rachel spoke in a tone both breezy and strained. She was referring to the pub, Thirsty Pelican, where they sometimes spent Friday evenings.

But Kimberley wasn't ready to absolve Rachel just yet. She couldn't allow her to get away with this: to start a doomsday countdown and then just waltz back in and stop the clock by asking, "Where's the party?" No, no, no. In a court of justice, Rachel would have to allocute, to spell out her apology. Kimberley was saying all this when Rachel cut her off. "*Cor bleh*, I did get on like a real cunt, eh. Last night, how I come at you. Sorry, babes. Let we just forget it and got a good time tonight, nuh. That's what we really need right now."

Kimberley smiled and picked up a pen, started sketching on the legal pad. "What we *need*, Rach?" she said. "Ain't you didn't *need* the scrambled eggs I make this morning? Instead, you leave with your face twist-up, like I make you suck lime for breakfast."

In the dead air, she heard Rachel's struggle for a comeback. Poor thing was never good at witty repartee, and when she gave up and burst out laughing, Kimberley found herself laughing too. And when Rachel said, in a voice crackling with emotion, "Never mind all that, I always goin' need you," Kimberley caved.

Who else would ever say that to her?

"An hour," she said, adding some tiny squares of light to the engorged heart she'd been drawing. "I'll meet you there."

When she plopped her brief-bag onto the front seat of the BMW, Kimberley was in a much better mood. She'd convinced the managing partner not to issue the legal opinion until Monday, claiming she needed to check some case-law at the Supreme Court. Rachel was at the bar—she'd already called twice more—and Kimberley was excited to see her and have the scare of the past twenty-four hours put behind them.

She slid her phone into the dashboard holster and swung out of the law firm's lot. Not even two streets away, it rang again and she pressed the answer button without looking.

"Good God, woman. So I tell you 7:00 and you call back at 7:01? You serious?"

Silence. Then "Kimberley," spoken by her mother's glacial voice. "Why haven't you called?"

"Mom?" she asked, her mind blank.

"Your father's been shot and you don't call? He's a politician so I'm sure it's been on the news there."

"What? How?" Her muscles seized.

"Last night. Do you really not know what happened?"

"A robbery? Is he dead?" Kimberley swerved the car and parked alongside the Parliament building. A shadow in the guard's booth moved and she imagined ski-masked bandits storming the cloth-store, kicking in the office door, demanding Mr. H open the safe. That could happen these days. Not in safe little Barbados, but back home, in bloody Trinidad. She pictured Mr. H trying to smooth-talk while reaching for his gun, his giant hands being too clumsy, in the end. The man was a troll, but she didn't want him dead. She leaned over the steering wheel and put her face within inches of the phone, as if that would help her comprehend what her mother was about to say.

"No, no," Mrs. H's voice got clippy, "it was a . . . young lady. He's at Santa Marta Private Hospital."

"Ohhhhhh," Kimberley said, flopping back into the seat. A tiny smile played on her lips. Mr. H being shot by a bandit—that would've been cruel. Mr. H being grazed by some little whore— that was comeuppance. "Well, good for her."

"Kimmy, don't be—"

"Really, Mother. You know he deserves it."

"Nobody deserves to be shot. I swear: you can be so selfish sometimes—just like him."

"At least the 'young lady' had the balls to do what you never could."

"Just come home. They say he's critical."

Kimberley didn't know what to do with the word "critical"— it was more than the bullet-graze she'd imagined. Part of her rushed out like a speedboat, but then stalled, drifting back to indifference—her usual mode whenever she thought of her father.

"Give me the number for the hospital. I'll call every day," she said. She swung the flap of her brief-bag and pulled out the legal pad, still open on that page with her heart-doodles, the pen clipping its side.

"He's your father. You can't really think that's good enough?"

Tired of Mrs. H's sarcastic questions, Kimberley decided it was time to ask some of her own. "Mother, was that fun for you? Wearing all those bruises?" she said, seeing in her mind's eye the fingerprints studding her mother's neck like a turquoise necklace. "Give me the number, please."

"If I can forgive him, why can't you?" Mrs. H said.

Kimberley pressed the pen into the page, going over the existing lines and curves of the heart, making them deep and thick. "You should call Miss Ivy too, Mother. I bet she'd be happy to know he's in critical—"

"Shut up! Don't talk to me about silly things you only half-remember."

A drop of water fell from Kimberley's nose, landed on the yellow page, making it swell.

"Silly? Silly, eh? And half-remember? No, Mother, I remember every detail."

Her ninth birthday party. The heel of her plastic, magical pony "high-heels" had broken off and she'd left everyone in the garden and trekked all the way back upstairs to change them. Miss Ivy, their housekeeper, was at the sink. Mr. H stood behind, squeezing her. Miss Ivy thrashed around—a black mouse in a trap—her head almost butting the metal faucet. She begged him, "Mr. H, no . . . Oh God, please. The Mrs. home . . ." Although Kimberley hadn't known exactly what was happening, she'd sensed that her father was taking something Miss Ivy wanted to keep, and she'd felt sad because she knew Miss Ivy would lose it anyway. Just like Mrs. H always lost to him. Women were cursed, Kimberley had decided then: their own bodies didn't even belong to them. She had run to her room and locked the door. Curled up, under her magical pony-and-rainbow sheets, she had prayed and prayed to fall asleep and wake up a boy. That way, she'd always belong to herself; other people might even belong to her. But Mrs. H came searching for her to rejoin the party. Kimberley told what she had seen and Mrs. H turned whiter, ghostly, but she'd dragged Kimberley back into the garden, whispering through gritted teeth, "You will forget what you saw, you will speak of it to no one, you will smile and finish off this party like a good hostess. Or so help me God, Kimmy, I'll throw away all those presents."

Now, Mrs. H was trying the same bullshit. "The point is, child: if your father dies you'll regret it. Besides, how would it look if you're not here? Your sister is flying eight hours from England; you can fly thirty minutes from Barbados. I've booked the ticket. Put your ass on that plane tomorrow at 5:00, okay?"

"I not coming!" Kimberley said, grabbing the phone from the holster and bringing it right to her lips, but Mrs. H had already hung up.

Tears blurred everything: the street, the inside of the car, Kimberley's own hand. She grabbed some tissues from the glove compartment, sopped her eyes and blew her nose. The legal pad still sat on her lap, heart all pock-marked with water, ink bleeding in places. It made Kimberley think of the graffiti that once covered her room—her Goth, teenage years. Mr. H had hated all the black, the heavy metal, the androgynous baggy clothes. "W'happen to all the kiss-meh-ass ponies?" he used to rail when he was drunk. "Them kiss-meh-ass ponies on rainbows?"

From the street, Kimberley glimpsed Rachel. At a cocktail table with some of their friends—Dexter, Carl and that crew—but a little too close to some girl in a yellow jumpsuit so tight it resembled an adult onesie. The girl's index finger wagged and wagged as she made some emphatic point, and Rachel was being persuaded; her frown and chronic nodding made that obvious. Kimberley had seen this chick circling Rachel before. Together, they looked like they were planning to rob the place.

She squeezed herself into the room and shouldered toward Rachel, moving on the same adrenaline that had piloted her car since Mrs. H's phone-call. She felt wide-eyed and giddy, desperate to get Rachel to the quieter side of the bar, to tell her about the shooting.

"Aye," she said, touching Rachel's elbow and waving at everyone else in the cluster.

"Hey!" Rachel replied, and as she bent for a cheek-press kiss, over her shoulder Kimberley glimpsed Yellow Onesie fleeing.

Why? She wondered, but had more urgent matters in mind.

"You actually make it," Rachel said, hand lingering on Kimberley's hip.

"You not gonna believe what happened," Kimberley said, nudging the hand away, a gentle reminder of the rules of public engagement.

"Tell me, nuh?" Rachel beamed. Yet Kimberley found herself standing there, tongue-tied. Her lawyer-senses took over and she foresaw that Rachel might ask about facts and emotions Kimberley didn't quite have. Not yet. Everything about her father being shot was still a swirling, black slurry in her mind.

She had to say something, though. So she embellished the story about the legal opinion and how she'd tricked her boss.

Rachel laughed and said, "After all that, you need a drink,

babes," then grabbed Dexter's arm, propelling him toward the bar.

Kimberley flashed a smile around, exchanged a few words with others in the group, nodded her head, tapped her feet, tried to enjoy the soca music—new catchy stuff from last month's Carnival in Trinidad. But she felt tired and locked out of all the merriment, as if she was still in the parking lot looking at everyone through plate glass. She'd told her mother she wasn't getting on that flight to Trinidad and in her head, playing in a loop, were all the reasons why she was justified. And yet, she felt a niggling doubt. A stray bit of shrapnel, spiraling, etching a tiny but painful track inside her chest. But she was determined not to notice the ache. Thank God, Rachel and Dexter were weaving back to the table.

Through swords of light and tendrils of smoke, Rachel moved, like a celebrity. Everyone eyed her, while she eyed Kimberley. Their misunderstanding was over, they were Soulmates With Benefits once more. Rachel handed Kimberley a cup of fries; everyone cheered Dexter for balancing the tray of tequila shots all the way from the bar; the group raised glasses; somebody did a countdown and then Kimberley licked the salt, tossed the golden liquid down her throat, and bit hard into a piece of lime. She shuddered at the taste, but felt alert again. Alert enough to focus. On getting drunk. On forgetting.

After tequila came vodka and they clashed beautifully. Just what Kimberley needed: her mind loose, stumbling around. Unfortunately, it collapsed on the doorstep of an unsolved mystery: that girl, Yellow Onesie. Why had she run away earlier? Why did she keep glancing over all night? What had Rachel told her about them? And it felt like more than a coincidence when, around nine-thirty, Kimberley stepped out of a bathroom stall at the same moment Yellow Onesie did.

They saw each other in the mirror. The music of the bar reverberated in the packed bathroom and yet they seemed to be alone in a bubble of suspicious silence. The girl smiled and Kimberley tried to, but it came out as a sneer.

They both reached for the paper towels. Yellow Onesie got there first.

"You and Rachel," she said, patting her hands, "you make a fine . . . team." Then she tossed the tissue and walked out, swinging her ass.

Kimberley rushed back to the table. Rachel was dancing with Dexter and Carl—a kind of three-person conga. Kimberley yanked her out and dragged her to the other side of the bar.

"What you tell that girl about us?"

"Who?" Rachel asked, wrenching her wrist away.

"Yellow outfit."

"Karen? Nuttin'."

"You lying."

"You paranoid."

For a few minutes, they stood there in the corner, behind a rubber plant, spitting insults in each other's faces.

"Okay, okay," Rachel said, finally. "I did need to talk to somebody and she understan'. She's the onliest body that understan' this problem we in."

"And what problem is that?" Kimberley shifted her weight from leg to leg, like a boxer squaring up.

"Same type of relationship, nuh. So she know how it feel."

"How what feels? Careful, eh."

Rachel took the dare. "To be somebody nasty li'l secret," she said, then dropped her eyes and fondled a rubber leaf, as if confirming its fakeness.

Kimberley clamped her palms against her temples, to stop her head from exploding. *This coming-out bullshit, again?*

And that word, *nasty*, and how Rachel had dragged it out, raking the past three years along with Kimberley's purest intentions through scum and sewer and then flinging them back in her face.

Kimberley couldn't bear it. She stabbed a finger—as hard as she could manage—into Rachel's breastbone, just above all that rosy cleavage, and said, "You can't play victim with me, girl. I know the truth about you."

"What I is, then? To you, Kim? And what's the truth? I listening. Go 'head."

One of Rachel's dreadlocks had sprung loose from the tie-back, and fallen onto her cheek. She dashed it away, hazel eyes blazing, never more beautiful or more repulsive to Kimberley. "The truth is, Rachel: you's just a kiss-meh-ass bully. Just like my father."

Kimberley left the bar.

After a long shower, she went out onto the balcony to smoke a cigarette and let the sea breeze slap her around a bit, sobering her. The apartment complex was quiet and dark. Even the sky seemed to be in OFF mode: no stars. A few boats bobbed in the distance, spaced out along the horizon like white traffic dashes on a black road to nowhere.

Kimberley had spent the whole hour thinking, about her father and about Rachel. Two currents, same gulf, they seemed. Both pulling her down to where she didn't want to go, but where she sensed all the missing answers were buried and rusting: her memory of the last day they'd all been together.

She and Rachel had been making breakfast when he'd banged on the door. Kimberley opened but he headed straight for Rachel, yelling, "Get out! Get out!"

Rachel had turned from the stove, looking to Kimberley for an explanation.

"I want this Bajan bitch out! Right now," he'd said. "No wickers on my property! That's what you Bajans call them, right? Take your despicable habits back to Barbados, young lady. And as for you, Kimberley, I sent you to school to be an attorney, not a big, fat, nasty queer."

"No, we're not . . ." Kimberley began. Rachel hadn't yet kissed her. She hadn't yet taken Kimberley's wide, awkward hand and guided it down to the narrowness between her legs. None of that had happened yet. They were innocent.

Yet Mr. H cut Kimberley off. "Save it," he said, "I own this shittin' place, I know everything that happens here. And for godsake, you let the maid find you together? You know how those nigger-people talk. By now, the news must be all over Pleasantview."

That's when Kimberley understood his accusation. A couple days before, she and Rachel had been up late, eating popcorn and watching DVDs. They'd fallen asleep right there, on her bed, and that's where the maid had found them the next morning, entangled.

Kimberley tried to explain this to Mr. H but he grabbed Rachel's arm, dragging her toward the door, saying, "They'll use this, Kim, mark my words. You will make me a laughing stock in Pleasantview, you stupid cow!"

Peeling his fingers from Rachel proved impossible; he was too strong. So Kimberley grabbed the broom and, for a millisecond, she did hesitate, but then she struck him hard on the collar-bone. With a howl, he released Rachel and swatted Kimberley halfway across the room. Everything happened in slow motion next: Rachel crawling across the tile, lifting the hem of her nightie, dabbing Kimberley's lip, printing bright red spots on Tweety Bird's faded feet.

"I want her out. Today," Mr. H had panted over them, mouth wet, face rabid.

Kimberley's insides had roiled as if she were on the verge of a diarrhea.

"If she leaves, I going too!" she had sputtered, the words salty with tears, snot and a little blood.

"Do it," Mr. H had warned as he stalked off, "and you're dead to me, young lady."

He'd left the door wide open.

The click-clacking of the locks made Kimberley startle.

Rachel was home from the pub. Although Kimberley felt softer toward her now, after reliving that memory, she didn't want to talk just yet.

Please head straight to your room! But no . . . kitchen noises: water gushing, china rattling, kettle gurgling. For what felt like forever, Kimberley sat there in hostage mode, staring at the balcony curtains, willing them not to betray her. Then, a gust lifted the gauzy panels into the living room, caused them to curl and beckon like fingers and not long after that, Rachel stepped out onto the balcony.

Kimberley got up and walked to the railing. The wind had died and the sea had returned to a patient mumble. She needed to speak first now, to control the conversation. "Dad was shot last night," she said into the blackness before her.

Rachel's chair—or maybe the table—screeched. "You mekkin' sport?"

Kimberley turned, but her hands clutched the railing behind her. She took a deep breath and told Rachel about the phone call from Trinidad.

Rachel set her teacup down. "I so, so sorry," she said, flapping her hands as if she were overheating and needed to self-cool. "That's what you was trying to tell me? Earlier, nuh?"

When Kimberley nodded, Rachel rushed over, hugged her, whispered more sorries, then led her inside to the couch, pulled her down and cradled her head. The touch was innocent and undemanding. Kimberley closed her eyes and tried to let every hard feeling dissolve in the warm silence between them. They had survived so much together.

"So when you leaving?" Rachel asked, twisting a curl of Kimberley's hair.

"I'm not."

"But you just say he critical."

"I'll see him at the funeral."

"You mad? He's your father."

"After how he's treated you . . . us . . . why are you on his side?"

"What the rasshole! The man deadin'. This ain't 'bout tekkin' sides, Kim."

"You sound just like Mom."

"But—"

"Look," Kimberley said, raising herself and her voice, "it's *my* father, *my* conscience, so thanks for your concern, but I can make my own decisions."

Rachel bared her palms in surrender. "Awright, I can't force you," she said. "Whatever you choose, babes."

Kimberley lay back down and they settled again, Rachel twirling Kimberley's hair and rubbing fingertips into her scalp. Kimberley shut her eyes and felt her whole blunt bulk lifting and floating with each breath. She was one of those boats out there, lolling in the tide, seaweed trailing and caressing its sides.

"Life so fleckin' short, eh?" Rachel interrupted. "I cyah imagine Daddy gettin shot. Or Mummy dyin' so sudden. Them is the onliest thing I love in this life—and you, of course. Nobody else. Please, Kim, let we just go tomorrow, nuh? Let we just do that *one* thing for now. I ain't goin' say nuttin. I promise, babes."

Kimberley was tired. She didn't want Rachel to pull away. More than anything, she wanted to be smothered, until she couldn't breathe, until she blacked out and forgot herself, her mother, her father—every damn thing in Trinidad. She reached up for Rachel's neck and drew her down.

"Okay," she whispered as they kissed, "Whatever you want."

Lunch had been pleasant and light-hearted—no pressure at

all—and it was difficult not to like Rachel's modern parents: Mrs. Clark, a kaftan-loving Swede who taught Feminist Studies at the University, and Mr. Clark, a stately black man—a dentist—who grew taller every time Rachel said "Daddy".

After they had cleared the dishes into the kitchen, Rachel smacked Kimberley's ass with a tea towel and said, "Let we go for a walk, nuh?" and Kimberley agreed.

They picked their way down some steep stairs to the beach and, on the last crooked step, Rachel grabbed Kimberley's hand, counted to three and ordered, "Jump!" They raised a puff of white sand as they landed, then Kimberley chased Rachel to the shade of a coconut tree.

They sat, catching their breath on a sun-bleached log, while Rachel coiled and coiled the pendant on her coral necklace—something she only did when she was nervous. Kimberley was about to ask what was wrong when—*Duff!*—a coconut dropped from the tree. They both ducked at the sound, and Kimberley cringed inside because it reminded her of Rachel's head hitting the floor on Thursday night.

"You think we should move?" she asked, but no answer came.

"I tellin' them," Rachel blurted out. "Now that we here and I see you with them, Kim, I know is the perfect time. Let we just do it."

Kimberley grabbed a stick and began drawing on the sand. Her heart and mind raced but went in different directions. She found herself tracing a big smiley-face, perhaps to distract from her own face, which she could not trust to convey the right reply to Rachel. What was the right reply? She flung the twig away and made her eyes scour the beach for some anchor, some mooring.

There! A woman on the jetty to their far left, the breeze on her long-sleeved blouse made her appear to be shivering. Or there! A tall, Nordic-looking woman strutting toward them, topless, her areolas like red cocktail umbrellas. This kind of exposure could only happen in Barbados, never, ever in Trinidad.

"Let's do it," Rachel repeated.

Kimberley spoke, then, in a strangled voice, "You promised me." She wasn't angry—which surprised her—just scared; there was a gun to her head, it seemed.

"Is the onliest way we goin' be happy, babes. We gotta be together in the open now,"

"But I don't need that, Rach. All I need—"

"But you love it, though." Rachel made a fist on Kimberley's thigh, and beat out a rhythm as she continued, "Yeah, when you lickin' and fingerin' me. *Cor blimey!* You love that cunt! You does try to hide whenever you comin'; you think I don't know . . . but I know, yes. You love it. You's a bare feckin' wicker, just like me. Admit it!"

"Is that bitch from the pub, right?" Kimberley knocked Rachel's hand away. "Karen? She's putting you up to this? You fuckin' her or what? Don't tell me you're so stupid you can't see what she's trying to do to us?"

"No," Rachel said, "You's the problem, Kimberley. Three fleckin' years: waitin' for you to stop hidin' yourself, waitin' for you to be ready. That finish. I tell you: I ain't hidin' nuttin' no more. I ain't waitin' again."

She got off the log and stood over Kimberley.

With upturned hands, as if the air around them was collapsing, Kimberley pleaded, "What you want from me, girl?

Blood? I can't!"

Rachel glared down, silent and goddess-like with the sun behind her; only her tears moved. Kimberley tried to match the stare, but looking up like that, into the light, made her eyes sting and weep. She lowered them to the turquoise sea, a glistening sheet of glass that stretched out to oblivion.

Rachel moved, offering her hand. "Are you coming?" she said. Her face, craggy and foreign. Her voice splintering as she added, "Please?"

A feeling swept over Kimberley, the same feeling she remembered from so long ago, when she'd watched her father with the sapodilla tree. A revelation, uncluttered by the fine print of life, of how deeply she loved this other failed human being. Then, in the same moment, the feeling seemed to crest and topple over on itself, draining away, as she glimpsed afresh the hopelessness of loving anyone that much, the inevitability of disappointment, the terrifying pain.

A knot loosened and something inside Kimberley slipped away and drifted off toward the horizon's sheen. She glanced at her watch, rising from the log as she whispered, "I going, Rach. I need to go back home."

Rachel began to cry some body-wracking sobs. "Is Trinidad you mean? You leaving me, Kim? You leaving me, nuh?"

Kimberley wrapped her arms around Rachel, rocked her as if they were slow dancing—right there, out on the open beach, for anybody to see. She didn't know if she was leaving Rachel. All Kimberley knew was that she could never live a new life, never have a new home, until she went back and spoke with her father.

She loved him. She needed to tell him—as soon as possible—and give him a chance to learn why the kiss-meh-ass ponies had died.

Loosed

"THAT'S WHAT YOU'RE WEARING?" RUTH ASKED.

Declan had known his wife would be watching, in her dressing-table mirror, as he left the bathroom. Watching, waiting to criticise. He'd known. And yet he went ahead anyway. He chose a pair of faded, ripped jeans and a green STAG T-shirt with the slogan—A MAN's BEER—in fat, white print. It was his opening salvo.

"What wrong with this?" He avoided Ruth's eyes as he sank to the bed to pull on his loafers.

"Declan, it's a church service. What will Bishop and the elders think?"

Left shoe on.

"Well, ain't the Bible say, 'Render your heart and not your garment'?"

Right shoe on.

"No, that's not what it—"

Declan sprang up. "Listen, my clothes wouldn't matter to Christ. Only to fake-ass Christians." He glared at the mirror, where their images were frozen. "So let's see which kind we dealing with tonight."

Today was their wedding anniversary. Ruth had asked him

to go with her to Night Service at Pleasantview First Holiness Revival Church, a Pentecostal circus just like the one his grandma used to drag him to as a boy. Ruth had often invited Declan to church. He'd refused every time. But today, he had to go.

Going to church together was what decent couples did to mark fifth anniversaries. This was what was expected. To not go tonight would be an outright announcement, to everyone in Pleasantview, that he and Ruth weren't the upstanding schoolteacher couple they appeared to be. He and Ruth had been the first in their families to earn degrees: he, Chemistry; she, English. They'd been the first in their families to get married—not like his sister, Judith, who'd shacked-up with her kids' father for seven years until he left to work in America. Declan and Ruth had been the first to move out of the ghetto—even if it was just across the traffic lights, to Hibiscus Park. Every time they went back to Pleasantview to visit friends and family, it was as if those people in the dark were seeing a great light. "Morning Miss, Morning Sir,"; everyone greeted them by their school-teacher titles. But it was hard being a shining example. And, every so often, it demanded a sacrifice. Like tonight.

"You know, Bishop predicted you would behave so," Ruth said, resuming whatever it was she did these days at her dressing table.

Declan stared at the reflection of his wife's face. A forty-two-year-old woman who no longer wore makeup, perfume, or jewelry. All those little tell-tale signs of effort, they signalled to a man that his woman still craved him. To Ruth's church, though, they signaled the sin of "vanity". Tonight, Declan would show those damn church-people how little he thought of them—they weren't even worth a pair of slacks and a dress-shirt—and he would expose them to his wife. He would use this opportunity to finally make her see: these "saints" were just plain old sinners in sheep's clothing. She was better off without them.

A few years ago, back when her name was still Michelle— she'd actually changed it because "hell" was in the middle—this business of getting dressed would've gone so differently. Declan would've readied himself first, then rushed into the living room to wait. He would've been watching TV half-heartedly, eager to see her emerge from their bedroom, to see what she'd done this time. What dress? What hairstyle? What colour lipstick? What shoe—the slutty platforms that made her taller than him, or the black, strappy ones that made her feet look like they had on lingerie? His pulse would've matched the rhythm of her heels down the corridor. When she finally appeared in the living room, though, he would've played it cool, dragging his eyes from the TV. She would've stood in the usual spot—between the love seat and the single chair—where she knew he'd have an unobstructed view. Then she would've asked casually, "You ready, Deck?" He would've smiled and nodded with his reply, "Not as ready as you, babes."

Now, he dropped his eyes from the mirror and walked over to the dresser for cologne. Ruth held the bottle out, as if she was doing him some great favour. He took it, making sure not to touch her hand. He wished he could, though, and wished that, by that one touch, he could exorcise Ruth completely from Michelle's body. *Then* he would have a reason to go to church and he would hold her hand the whole time, thank Jesus with all his heart, then take her to dinner afterwards. A fancy knife-and-fork dinner, just like old times.

God knows, he and Ruth hadn't gone out together in what? Years: two, three, maybe?

He knew the things people said, how they called him "understanding" for letting Ruth pursue her "path" even though he "believed differently". The truth was Declan had been betting all along that Ruth's faith was unsustainable—an experimental flash of fire, like that trick he did in the science lab: potassium permanganate and glycerin. *Poof!* Over.

With time, though, an uninvited blackness, like mold, had over-run his hope. This might not be a passing phase. This might be a transmutation. His wife, Michelle, might be permanently gone. In her place, this Bible-thumping freak named "Ruth".

"Why you have to be such a damn groupie all the time?" Declan snarled at her. "Who cares what your precious Bishop predicted? Ain't we agree I could wear anything I want?"

He had sensed himself growing desperate lately, as this fifth anniversary approached. He hadn't known what to do about it, right up until fifteen minutes ago when he was in the shower. That's when he decided tonight was *the* night. He would bring Michelle back—shock her, talk sense into her, ridicule her—he'd take action, tonight.

"Yes, but I didn't expect something so . . . demonic," Ruth replied, stabbing another pin into the coil of hair at her neck. She seemed to flinch and then bleed a smile—just for a nanosecond—at each stab, like she was enjoying a medieval penance. Declan let out a long, juicy steups and left the bedroom. This was why he needed his outside-woman, Trudy:

a normal, sane female to balance off this madness.

In the corridor, he had a wicked thought that made him veer into the living room to squint at the CD rack. Ah! There: "Dancehall Mix". A disc he'd bought on a whim, about a year ago, at the Pleasantview traffic-lights, from a scraggly boy named Silence. Declan had listened to it scornfully at first, had endured the merciless bass, the cussing, the crudeness: punani this, cocky that, ride-ride-ride, fuck-fuck-fuck. It wasn't really his thing: he was a smooth, sophisticated man; a jazz-and-R&B kind of guy. He kept listening to this CD, though, because at the time, he'd felt like he needed to. All over Pleasantview, young fellas were in their cars pounding out these styles; and in clubs, pushing up on girls to these beats; and in their tiny bedrooms, stinky with sweat, sports, semen and never-washed sheets, banging girls to these rhythms. Declan used to be one of those invincible boys. But at forty-three, the way his life was going with Ruth, he'd felt he needed to borrow some of that fire, to remember what it was like to be ablaze.

The CD had stayed in Declan's car for about a month, became the soundtrack of his drives to and from school. The "fucks" stopped grating and he learned the other lyrics without even trying. Then one afternoon, Trudy, the much-younger-History-teacher-with-no-man, had car trouble so he offered her a ride. The music came on full blast and she looked at him like he was a pervert, like she was ready to report him to the Principal. Declan had fumbled with the volume knob and eject button. "Sorry, sorry," he'd stuttered, tempted to crack the disc in two. Trudy had smiled in a pouty way and said, "You're versatile, *Mister* Rochard." It was a dare: you're old, but are you cold?

Declan plucked the disc from the shelf and headed to the car to wait for Ruth. So, he was demonic? Fine then. He would go to Night Service with her but, on the way, he'd teach her what demonic really sounded like. Fuck her, fuck the Bishop, fuck all the elders.

They pulled up to the Pleasantview traffic lights and the same Silence was there—selling mangoes this time. Declan raised the volume on the CD player, honked and waved at the boy like they were old friends. All for Ruth's benefit. To show how unaffected he was by her pinched face. Silence was just about to run across to them with a bag of fruit when the light changed and Declan sped off. Ruth reached down, lowered the music.

For spite, Declan drove badly. He sang and worked the pedals to make the car dance. When Track 5 began, he swiveled the volume knob and sang louder, "*Gyal, skin out! Say if you know you can take the wuk. Gyal skin out!*" He sliced eyes at Ruth. Skin out? Did she even remember how to? She walked around like a rusty clothespin, like she couldn't open her legs even if she tried. Which is why he didn't blame himself for anything. He was a normal, hot-blooded man. It was *she* who'd stopped sleeping with *him*.

Declan remembered the exact day. Two years ago, at a time when things weren't yet so bad between them. Ruth had barged through the door one Sunday after church. "Bedroom. Now!" she'd ordered, as she kicked off her shoes and ran upstairs. He'd left the TV and followed, taking the steps two by two, thinking the worst: another round of bleeding, clots, loss, grief. A grief that made the house seem too small; it bundled them into opposite dark corners.

"What? W'happen?" he asked breathlessly, lunging into the bedroom.

Ruth was stripping, like her clothes were full of red ants. She explained between pulls and tugs, "Healing service today. Bishop laid hands on me, Deck. He say before the anointing leave my body, we should try again. You drink beers today?"

"No. But you believe that old-talk, girl?"

"Good, then you ain't defile yourself. Come on, I ready." Ruth was now naked.

She climbed onto the bed and lay with her legs and arms spread wide, curly hair fanning out. Like that famous da Vinci drawing, Declan thought. Like she was submitting herself in the service of science. It wasn't sexy. But he'd tried anyway, and failed. Who wouldn't? Which man alive could stay hard if he knew that his woman didn't really want him, that she was thinking about and whispering the name of another man? There Declan was, trying to pelt waist; and there she was, whispering, "Jesus . . . Oh Jesus . . . Come, Lord Jesus."

Ruth seemed to hate Declan more after that failure. It was as if he'd lost all usefulness to her. She'd moved into the spare bedroom that same evening.

Hurt afresh by the memory, Declan mashed the accelerator and swung the volume dial almost to its highest. Ruth turned it back down again. He swung it back up.

"Declan," she said, "please stop. Please. Can't you just put everything aside, just for tonight? It's our anniversary. Can't you just do this for me? Please?"

It was the "for me" that got Declan. That and her voice cracking. He still loved her—well not this version of her, not Ruth. He loved Michelle. God, how he missed her! The last time Declan had seen her was on Carnival Tuesday three years ago. As usual, they'd played mas in the band, Harts. They liked to play in the same section, but pretend they weren't together. Carnival was a time to be free: he could wine-up on any woman; she could grind-up on any man. Of course, it was difficult for Declan to watch his wife in her costume—for all its sequins and feathers it was really just a bra, thong and stockings—and just surrender her luscious, bouncy ass to all mankind. But to see her flailing, cheeks red from sun and rum, hips gyrating, eyes closed in the ecstasy of soca music; and to watch other men watching her, jockeying to be the one who got closest, the one who got to thief a wine on her ass—it made Declan feel other things. Good things. He was the one who'd be taking her home and he was the one who'd be making love to her that night and every night.

Except that three years ago, on that Carnival Tuesday night, she left him for Jesus.

Since then, Declan passed his days in a tug-o'-war between the looming suspicion Michelle was gone forever and the tiny hope she was still alive, somewhere, buried inside this holier-than-thou Ruth. That all he needed to do was dig Michelle out. Most days, he just ignored his wife and waited for deliverance to come from somewhere; other days he reasoned that the right remark—sharp and cutting—would free her. But there were still other times, like now, when his wife spoke to him in this way— "please . . . for me . . ."—with this humility, Declan couldn't bring himself to keep up the nastiness. It sounded so much like an apology, like she knew she was the guilty one, like she was asking him to just bear with her a little while longer.

He switched the music off. A weighted silence took its place.

Just as it had that Carnival Tuesday night in the car, on the way home. Michelle had been so quiet that Declan had reached over and squeezed her thigh. She began to sob that she "just couldn't do it anymore"; she'd been "pretending to have a good time", but she "would never play mas again." All the way home, she'd sobbed and babbled while Declan tried to figure out what she meant. After a long bath—so long he'd knocked twice to see if she was still alive—Michelle had emerged into their living room, her long curly hair slicked back, her eyes bloodshot.

She sank onto the couch next to him and held his hand. She confessed that she had, since the last "bleeding episode", been studying The Word with Yolande and Ottley, who lived two doors down in Townhouse 4. When? On evenings while Declan played football. They'd invited her to Church and she'd gone. When? A couple of weeks ago, while he was at that weekend retreat with his students. She'd felt something move inside her during the service but she'd held back. Why? Carnival was around the corner and she knew how much Declan was looking forward to it and that he'd already paid for their costumes. She'd chosen to ignore God's call—she'd done it for Declan. But she couldn't live that empty life anymore. She'd made up her mind to get saved.

There were so many cars Declan had to park down the street. It was the second night of a seven-day crusade and a huge, red-and-white, Ringling Brothers-style tent occupied the church parking lot.

"Oh look, a circus!" Declan said as they left the car. He couldn't resist throwing some picong at Ruth.

She stuck her nose even higher in the air. She crunched away, through the gravel, toward a group of old ladies lurking in a huddle at the side of the stage. Declan guessed they were part of the choir. All fat; the long white robes and belts of golden braid made their stomachs look pregnant. They embraced Ruth, two by two, rocking her back and forth, side to side, patting her back as if she were a baby they were trying to belch. When was the last time she'd hugged him, her husband? Then he watched them turn like synchronized swimming whales, to scowl at him. What had she told them? What sad story was she telling them now? About his clothes? The music? Poor, poor Ruth; married to that terrible, terrible Declan. He smiled and waved as if he hadn't registered the bad vibes.

In truth, now that Declan was actually here, he did feel awkward in his STAG T-shirt. Like a child wearing a superhero costume to a wedding—then regretting it. Everyone seemed to be pointing at him. *Awww . . . a soul in need*, their faces seemed to say.

Declan squared his jaw and looked around for something to criticize. The place was shabby; it seemed Bishop had spent all the tithes-and-offerings on the Audi parked outside. Imagine: Ruth gave that joker ten percent of her monthly salary—ten percent that could help with the mortgage Declan was now carrying alone, like a friggin' cross. A few feet away, under the glare of some precariously hung fluorescent lights, two youths in shirt-and-tie wrestled with rusty folding chairs. Another boy stood under one of the lights with a broom, sweeping the bulbs, trying to coax them to light from end to end. A few decades ago, that might've been Declan. In the Jumping-Jesus church just like this one, where his grandma had worshipped. There was always one in Pleasantview—taking poor people's money to fatten the pastor, giving false hope in return. Where was the pastor and all that money when Declan's grandpa had died? When his grandma, in her sixties, had to start scrubbing shit out of other people's drawers to make ends meet? When, on the worst days of Mammy's arthritis, Declan and his sister, Judith, had to fight-up with the brown stains themselves?

Declan's pulse pounded with rage and shame. He had to look away from the boy.

At the front of the tent, a small plywood stage had been erected, made smaller by a massive carved podium. Gargoyles eating grapes, it looked like—but it could just as well have been angels. Who knew with these superstitious freaks?

Ruth's voice came from behind, startling him, "Bishop says they have seats for us in front. Come, nah."

Declan considered pointing out that she was breaking another part of the deal they'd made about tonight. They were supposed to lay low near the back, where he could slip out now and then when he needed fresh air, or when he couldn't stand any more of the somersaults and vampire-slaying brought on by the Holy Spirit. But Ruth stood before him, chewing her cuticles. Declan felt afresh that pinch of regret about the T-shirt and the music in the car. He followed her to the front row.

He made it through the scripture reading and opening prayer. He even maintained his smile when the Deacon reminded everyone of the night's theme: "Saving Marriages, One Soul at a Time." That's when Declan glanced around and noticed the male-female-male-female seating configuration: the audience was composed of couples.

He grunted and locked his arms across his chest, debating if to feel tricked or not. Ruth had made it sound like an ordinary Night Service, like they were just coming to pray; she hadn't mentioned the sermon would be focused on marriage. But then again, Declan considered, this *was* appropriate for a couple celebrating their fifth anniversary. And by now, Ruth surely knew better than to think she could convert him. What she didn't know, Declan smirked inwardly, was that he was intent on *her* re-conversion—back to Michelle—tonight.

He began his crusade by whispering in her ear. "So, how much you think that Audi cost? . . . Papayo! That's a fancy suit Bishop wearing there. What colour that is? Pimpish-purple? . . . Any young girls pregnant for him yet?"

Over and over, getting nastier and nastier, Declan peppered Ruth for almost an hour, and yet she ignored him.

She was jubilant during Praise-and-Worship: jumping, waving, prancing— it wasn't an act or something she was doing just to annoy him. And when they sang "Roll, Jordan, Roll," the woman was practically rolling her waist! Declan hadn't seen her so animated since that last Carnival Tuesday. A whirring sound, an unsettling sensation, came over him, as if he was trapped in a centrifuge. Something gritty swirled in his stomach, while something liquid rose to his chest. He felt nauseous. Maybe it was the crowd—being packed in, shoulder to shoulder, like that; he'd always been a little claustrophobic.

Ruth danced, and the more she did, the more seasick he felt, the more he gnawed inside his cheek. But Declan couldn't look away. If only she would stop moving. If only she wouldn't glow so much. If only she didn't seem so alive.

He grabbed her underarm and reeled her in. "This is what you does come here for? To wine like you in a fête?"

Ruth wrenched free, continued rejoicing. Somewhere between "Shout to the Lord" and "Make a Joyful Noise", it hit Declan that he'd always known this but had never wanted to actually see it and have his suspicions confirmed: Ruth was far different with these people than she was at home; she was happy. She'd taken something that was once his and given it to these strangers. It was the worst betrayal he'd ever known. He'd tried to even the scales—Trudy—but that had never made him as happy as Ruth was now. A pang of loneliness, like a sudden foul smell, made his eyes sting and burn.

Testimonies started and Declan was relieved they could finally sit. Over a crackling, wheezing sound-system people droned on about how the Lord had changed their lives for the better. Declan forgot himself for a bit as he listened. Sex, drugs, booze, kleptomania—gripping stuff! These people seemed, to Declan, eager to prove some kind of scientific correlation between how sinful they were in the past and how much Jesus loved them now. It was especially hard not to laugh at the illiterates, like the man who testified he was a born-and-raised Hindu but his life changed the day he'd heard the story of "The Portugal Son", and the dougla lady who claimed she was a former prostitute but, even in those days, between jobs, she'd studied "The Book of Palms".

These testimonies comforted Declan. Yes, he had Trudy, but he'd never been as depraved or as foolish and reckless as any of these folks. He was a good, educated, respectable man.

"You see?" he said, nudging Ruth's ribs. "You call me a demon for wearing a T-shirt and playing a CD, but I never yet do anything like these people, your so-called friends."

Ruth answered from the side of her mouth, not taking her eyes off the stage. "At least they're not hiding anything."

"I not hiding anything," he said.

It had suddenly become noisy as, next to them, Sister Yolande was prattling in tongues.

"Oh really? Then prove it. Why you don't go up?" Ruth shout-whispered in his ear.

It took Declan a moment to realise she was referring to the Altar Call the Bishop had just made, for any spouse who wished to be "born again".

"Look, girl, don't be stupid," he said, then turned his back to her.

As he faced the open side of the tent, a cool night breeze reached him. He leveled his arm on the back of the chair, propped his head and closed his eyes. He longed to be released.

A brain-splitting squeal came from the speaker-boxes at the front. Declan jerked upright and stuck his fingers deep into his ears. He turned around just in time to see Bishop Roystone T.

Scantlebury—with jerri-curls alive like mercury—descending from the stage. The Bishop shimmied and danced on the first stair, grimacing with holy passion till his unibrow convulsed—but a worm in a beaker of acid is what Declan saw.

Scantlebury gargled his words, like Listerine, before spitting them out so hard every line ended in the same phonetic syllable.

"...And Gahd said to me-ah,

He said 'Roystone-ah,

I'm about to give you a word-ah,

For a special woman here tonight-ah.'"

There, Bishop paused, giving the congregation time to cheer. Some clapped, some stamped their feet, some swayed.

He hopped to the middle step and continued. "This word is for a woman unevenly yoked, tied to a man who don't know Jesus. Sister, no matter what you do, your man just won't believe. You know why?"

"Why?" came the high-pitched response. All the women in the audience were yelling in unison but, seated next to Ruth, Declan heard only her plaintive voice. He stole a glimpse at her. She sat there gaping at the Bishop, unblinking, as tears spilled onto her cheeks. She was thinking about them, wasn't she? Her face, her tears—just like that awful evening, that last time, when he'd come home from work and found her on the toilet, crying. He'd known right away she'd lost another one. And now, just as then, Declan's forearm twitched with the urge to pull out his kerchief and wipe her face, but he was afraid to touch her.

The Bishop was now on the last stair. "See, your husband is a man afflicted. Blame the Devil, sister! Don't you blame your man! For, no matter his faults, the Bible says he is still the head of your household."

"Amen! Amen!" the baritone voices took over. Declan was silent. He hadn't acted like the head of anything when he'd remained at the bathroom door and urged his wife, "Come on, stop crying. We'll get through this one too," before escaping to their bedroom and locking the door behind him, locking her out.

As if she was sharing in the memory, Ruth turned to Declan and met his eyes. His impulse was to break the stare but he found he couldn't. They hadn't looked, really looked, at each other in ages. He saw no disdain or judgment in his wife's gaze—only a skewed silhouette of himself stretched over her dark pupils. He stared past it, as if down a tunnel, searching for Michelle. And he thought he glimpsed her—her love at least— she was still there, hovering, misty. What was *she* reading in *his* eyes? Love, shame, the truth he couldn't say: that he'd left her in the bathroom because he'd felt his body folding in on itself like a broken umbrella, and that he'd ended up in a heap on the bedroom floor, crying too, because after three lost babies he was angry with her, and with God, for putting him through a fourth.

Now, Declan dared not breathe. The movement of his chest might interrupt whatever it was taking place between him and his long-lost Michelle. Was this the moment she'd come back and forgive him? He wanted permission to forgive himself.

Then Bishop made landfall, and bellowed into the microphone,

"Gahd says, 'Woma-a-an!

Thou art loosed-ah!

I will finish the good work-ah

I have begun in you-ah!

And tonight-ah,

And forever more-ah,

I will loose your man!'"

Ruth ripped her eyes from Declan's and launched from the chair, bawling openly now, waving both arms at the Bishop as if he were a rescue plane.

Declan jumped up as well, a reflex. For the past three years they'd been castaways on opposite sides of the same empty island but now, now that they'd finally made contact, he could not let her leave. Not again. He wanted to shout, "Michelle! Look at me! Me! Not Scantlebury! We don't need him." But Declan stood foolishly, arms dangling when he knew they should be reaching.

Garbled instructions were being yelled over the mic and Declan lost sight of the Bishop. The open space between the front row and the stage grew dark with jostling bodies. For a moment, the crowd seemed to swallow Ruth, but then she burst through and flung her arms around Declan, stapling their bodies together.

The circle contracted and, it seemed, a thousand hands fell upon him. Thud after thud shook his back. He wriggled, but couldn't free himself. The centrifuge started spinning again. He heard nothing but a dull roar, saw nothing but shadows. Then, Bishop Scantlebury's face appeared. Ruth let go but the Bishop's abysmal glare held Declan in place. He planted a palm on Declan's forehead and gave a mighty push. Or did he? Declan felt himself falling backwards but had no time to panic. He felt himself pass through arms and chairs and legs and reams of memories. All he knew when he hit the ground was that his wife was now on top of him. He was back in her arms.

Declan slowly came to. Where was he? Had he fallen asleep on the carpet in front of the TV? Above, one face: Michelle. She kissed his forehead. He lay still and smiled at his love, his eyes finding their focus.

Then she said, "Praise God," and Declan sat up as if released by a spring.

It was slow and fast at the same time: the remembering, the feeling of having his insides scalpelled out, of losing Michelle again. There was only Ruth, stroking his face and saying, "It's okay, babe. You were slain in the Spirit, praise God."

Grief, hot and red, rushed through Declan. He wanted to cry. He wanted to howl. He wanted to rip his clothes. He tried to stand. Yolande and Ottley rushed to help, cooing and lifting him by the underarms like a newborn. Declan shoved them away, handed Ruth the car keys and staggered out of the tent.

The CD player remained off. Ruth was driving. Her voice filled the car as she tinkle-tinkled like an over-wound ballerina, whirling to her own distorted melody.

Declan sat in the passenger seat, taut and still tightening. His mind strummed one chord, the same chord: apology, apology. *She* owed *him* an apology. For tricking him into attending the service, for having the pastor and her friends ambush him, for them crowding him till he couldn't breathe, or hitting him on his head—or whatever they'd done to get him on the floor like a blasted fool. For the past three years. For everything.

"So what did you see?" Ruth asked, reaching across to squeeze his hand.

"What?"

"When you were out? What did the Holy Spirit show you? The apostle John saw the whole of the Book of Revelation. There's no shame in it; you can tell me."

Declan withdrew his hand, gripped his knee.

"But some people don't see anything," she continued. "It doesn't really matter. What matters is that tonight, you received Jesus as your Lord and Saviour. When you were on the floor and I was holding you and Bishop asked, I heard you say yes. Things will be different for us now, Deck. You're a new man now."

The high green walls and electronic gate of Hibiscus Park came into view, about fifty feet ahead. Ordinarily, Declan would've picked up the gate remote by now. Forty feet. He would've pressed it by now. Thirty feet. But this time, he said, "Stop, stop, stop."

Ruth mashed down on the brakes, looking worried.

"Pull over and park," he said.

She did, then leaned toward him. "You want to throw up? That happens to some people after . . ."

Stabbing the switch for the overhead lights, Declan said, "At first, I really thought this was a phase, you know, Michelle."

At the sound of her old name, she recoiled into her seat.

"Yeah, for this conversation, you're Michelle—you can go back to being whoever you want after."

Declan felt he was sitting on top of something huge and

powerful, gripping its reins, trying to restrain it before it trampled them both into the mud.

Yet his wife stared at him exactly the way some of his students did in class, uncomprehending: forehead twisted and knotty. And, just as he did with them, Declan tried not to doubt himself.

"I thought it was all about that last . . . loss . . . after we were trying so hard. Maybe you thought God was punishing you? Or maybe you thought if you prayed harder He would do something for us? I didn't know for sure, but—"

"Did you ever ask?"

"Michelle, I ask you all the time why you're hiding in that Church!"

"No, did you ever ask me how I felt about what happened?"

"Well, I could see you were sad. That's natural. But, each time you got over it, went back to normal. I figured that last time would be the same. That's why I thought—"

"You blamed me, ain't? You decided something was wrong with me. You resented me," she said, voice quivering.

"Come on!" he urged through gritted teeth. He didn't want to answer that question, to put himself in the wrong. Not when he still had so much righteous steam to vent.

"Yeah," she said, her features curdling, "that's exactly what you said that last time. When I was on the toilet crying my guts out? You said that same thing: 'Come on', like I was being melodramatic."

Declan made a steeple with his fingers. "Michelle, you know I was disappointed too. I just meant we could try again. I didn't know what else to—"

"We did. Remember? At least *I* did. *I* tried again." She

looked past Declan, as if there was something out there behind him. He had to stop himself from glancing over his shoulder. "But anyway," she continued, "God knew what he was doing. You weren't ready to be a father; you could barely be a husband."

Declan grabbed the hand-brake. She was right but he didn't want to hear it out loud. From her, all he wanted to hear was sorry. With his thumb, he began a secret, manic clicking of the engage button. "Oh! Is so? Well, tonight your precious know-it-all Bishop said plenty 'bout being a proper wife. When last you behaved like that? When last you had sex with me?"

"When last you had sex with someone else? That is the question!" She flung the car door open and got out. For a few seconds, she stood there in the middle of the road, as if trying to decide what to do next. Then she headed for the pavement. As she rounded the front of the car, Declan leapt out and blocked her path.

He put his hands on her shoulders. She tried to shrug them off but Declan wouldn't let her. They began to struggle. Right there, under the street lamp, in the shadow of the mint green walls of Hibiscus Park, mere feet from their own gate. They wrestled and clawed at each other. Neither spoke, but breathy grunts escaped them as she pushed and he pulled. He got hold of her wrists and clamped them behind her back. She kept writhing, she was slippery, she tried to bite him—his chest—but then Declan felt her give up and go limp in his arms.

Cautiously, he let her go. She was panting. Her expression was softer than it had been in the car, her eyes milky. She shifted, her fingers landing like a butterfly on Declan's cheek as she said, "All this confusion, we could put it behind us now, Deck. Tonight changed everything. We should go inside and . . . be together. Whatever was wrong with you down there—it's healed."

Declan's hand shot out. He slapped his wife with a force that flung them apart: her against the bonnet of the car, him against the green wall. His eyes searched the pavement in a panic, as if it wasn't *he* who'd done it, as if there was some invisible, malevolent spirit to blame. But, no, they were alone. Declan turned from Ruth then, began stomping down the pavement, away from the car, back the way they'd come, toward Pleasantview. Soon, he was running, sprinting: chest up, fingers pointed, heart pounding. The closest place was his sister Judith's house. Small, cramped with her two boys, but tonight it would do. God! What Ruth had done to him in the Church! What he'd just done to her! Declan knew he had to go. He had to leave the townhouse tonight, tonight, tonight. He had no choice. He no longer knew the people who lived there.

Six Months

WHEN OIL DROP TO 9US$ A barrel, man, you know you getting lay off. The only question is when. Like everybody else in the industry, you wait.

It come like the worst thing that could happen, when they announce people going "in tranches" every month.

At first, every time you don't get a envelope, you breathe a sigh of relief. After a while, though, you start feeling like a death-row inmate in a cell near the gallows; like these bitches want you to witness everybody else execution. Soon, the fact you still working come like a noose swinging in front your face, grazing your nose. You start to wish they just get it over with.

And when it happen, you rush home to Judith, your common-law wife, mother of your two children, and give her the news. She put her hand on her heart and say, "We could breathe easy now, Junior. We could move on."

You and Judith cling to each other there in the kitchen. You feel your prick resurrecting like Lazarus. Is months since the last time. You know Judith feeling it too. She pulling away? No, she gripping on tighter.

You's a trembling schoolboy again, mouth watering over hers as you grab deep inside that housedress like is a bran tub.

You find her panty-crotch and rake it aside. Right there on the counter, next to the toaster, it happen. Two jook and a tremble and everything done. But Judith don't seem to mind. She patting your back, stroking your hair, till your breathing slow down. Then she whisper she going for the boys.

You swagger to the bedroom. Dive on the bed, hug the pillow, and smile. You not too worried. The severance pay was a good chunk—it'll hold you for a while. Besides, you tell yourself, it don't matter how low oil go; Trinidad need man like me. They can't shut down every rig, every factory. Nah! METs will always find work.

But then April turn to May, May turn to June, and still nobody hiring Mechanical Engineering Technicians. The talk everywhere is recession, recession. Judith still have her receptionist job in the doctor-office and y'all could probably manage a li'l while longer. But what really starting to hurt is your pride. You's a big, hard-stones man and watch you: every day, waking up with the house empty and a note from Judith on the table. Cook, clean, wash, iron—you do everything she say.

Until one night, when Judith squat over your face and say "suck it," you shove her off and say, "Suck it your damn self. I's not your bitch."

You call your cousin Rufus, in New York. America have the most factories. Rufus name "citizen"; he must know somebody to offer you something under the table.

Three days later, he call back. Good news. If you organize your visa and ticket and get there by September month-end, they'll squeeze you in at the S-Town Supermarket near his house in Queens. "Engineering work?" you say. And the man say no, is the meat room. You tell Rufus, "Yeah," but, same speed, you hang up and tell Judith, "He mad or what? I have education!"

You plan to wait couple weeks, then say you didn't get the visa. Meantime, you drop your tail between your leg and call your eighteen-year-old baby sister, Gail.

"You think you could ask that old man something for me?"

"A job, nah?" Gail say, like she was waiting on the call.

"Yeah, girl. Things hard. You know I's not the kind to ask Mr. H for favors. But them Syrians, they own everything. See what you could do, nah?"

Imagine *you* asking Gail for help. After you never do one ass for her. After you did move out and leave her with that drunk skunk, your father, Luther Sr.

When she first hook up with Mr. H, that married asshole, it did make you feel to vomit: your li'l sister spreading her legs for him, for his money. You did tell Judith as much and she say, "Well, talk to Gail. You's she big brother."

But you did say, "Nah, is not my place." And is true. Gail was fuckin' for betterment. How you coulda ever face her and say, *Don't*, when Mr. H was the one minding her: putting a roof over she head, food on she table, clothes on she back, making she feel classy, giving she a start in life. That's more than you— Mr. Big Brother—or your waste-a-time father ever do for the li'l girl. *Shame!*

Next day, Gail call back: "Sorry, boy. Hard luck."

You wonder if she even ask.

One night, after everybody fall asleep, you packing away the school books your son Jason leave on the dining table. Flipping through his sketch pad, a heading in red catch your eye: "My Family." Four stick figures in scratchy crayon clothes. You's the tallest and next to your watermelon head it have a arrow and a label: "Luther Jr. Stay-at-home Dad." In your hand it have something that resemble . . . a axe? a boat paddle? Nah, you realize is a spatula.

"Fuck," you mumble, pulling out a chair and sinking in it. Your son gone and ask the teacher what to call you, now that you's scratch your balls for a living.

"Junior, you sure you want to do this?" Judith say. She straining macaroni in the sink; you grating cheese. "America ain't no bed-a-rose, nah!" she add.

You argue back and forth 'bout all the people she know that gone America and dying to come back.

Then—*thunk!*—Judith rest-down the strainer hard in the sink. You glance across. She staring out the window.

"You go miss me? That's what it is, ain't? Tell me."

"Don't be a ass!" she say. "I's a big woman, I could handle myself. But, is the boys . . ."

"Let we cross that bridge when we get to it," you say, a tightness in your chest like you just bench-press one-fifty. "I don't even have a visa yet."

You go down a li'l stronger on the grater. This fuckin' woman hard! Harder than this old, dry cheese. It woulda kill her to say she go miss you?

The two of you was seventeen, in the last year of technical

school, when she get pregnant with Jason. Y'all wasn't in love or nothing, but her granny put her out, so you had to band together. *Your* parents was a disgrace: Luther Sr. drowning in puncheon rum, and your mother, Janice, ups-and-gone with a next man. Three years pass you straight, like a full bus. Then Judith find out she pregnant again, with Kevin. You and Judith, it come like y'all grow up together. And, although you's a big man now, twenty-four years, you never had to face the outside world without Judith. She raise your babies and, in a way, she raise you too.

She never been the lovey-dovey kind but, man, she get more colder lately. She dropping words for you; saying things like, "People can't make love on hungry belly."

You pay for the appointment, fill out the form, take the picture. You photocopy a bank statement, fake a job letter. You line up in the road at 5:00 AM, in front the US Embassy, with a sandwich and a juice box in your jacket.

People in the line *shoo-shoo*-ing. Uncle Sam know everything is what they saying. Hmmm. Suppose the Embassy ask 'bout your aunt who did overstay her six months in LA? Suppose they know you lose your real job?

When your batch of twenty get call-in the Embassy, you watch everything. People go up once to hand in their documents. Then again for the interview. You figure out those getting send by the Post Office counter is the lucky ones. Them others, who drop their eyes and slink out quick, quick, them is the rejects.

You watch five from your batch get reject—some of them real posh-looking.

Shit! If they could do them that, who's me? You feeling like you have to pee but you dare not leave your seat.

At 9:00, they call your name; 9:15, the interview start.

The lady barely watching you. She asking simple questions but you feel like she just waiting for you to trip up. When she ask, "Purpose of visit?" you amaze yourself with how you slant the lie you and Judith did practice ("Vacation"). How you pull it nearer the truth.

"School purchases," you say in your best English, "before September. The children needs plenty things."

The lady smile. "They always do," she say.

Your B1/B2 visa get approve.

You feel high and light—like you could reach America on your own fuckin' wings. You stop at KFC, near City Gate, and splurge: a bucket, four regular sides, a two-liter Sprite. A nice surprise for the boys after school. On the maxi-taxi ride home, you decide how you going to tell them.

Jason ripping into his second piece. Kevin still nibbling a drumstick. You watch all their hand and face getting greasy and sticky; the ketchup plopping down on their vests. Scabby knee, shred-up elbow, Jason missing teeth, Kevin always-runny nose. Is like you recording a movie in your head, to replay later, in America. They sit, stand, climb, all over the dining-table chairs, while Judith complaining and wiping, wiping.

Finally, you say, "Boys, what if we could eat KFC every Friday?"

Not even glancing up from his meat, Jason answer, "I done ask Mummy that long time and she say we can't afford it."

"I know. But we could afford it now. Daddy going America."

The boys stare at you blank, blank.

"Allyuh have to make a list of all the toys allyuh want. Because, when I go America, I getting *everything*." You growl the last word, bare your teeth, like a hungry lion.

The cubs laugh.

"America far?" Jason say.

"Yes, I have to go on a big airplane."

"We could go too?"

"No, you have school. Plus you have to take care of your mother." You glance at Judith. She look like she holding her breath. In truth, you doing the same damn thing.

"So, Daddy," Jason say, "when you say 'everything' you mean I could get a G.I. Joe watch?"

The boys call toy after toy, snack after snack—everything they know from American TV. With every yes, their excitement grow and grow. Till they fidgeting again—more than ever now—popping up like bubbles in the Sprite. They start rocking the chairs and singing, "Daddy going America! Daddy going America!" They making you feel like you's a superhero.

"Stop it!" Judith shout. "Stop that right now!"

A few weeks later, in the purple-looking hours before dawn, you slink out your bed and into the boys' bedroom. You tiptoe and kiss Jason, on the top bunk; you bend and kiss Kevin, his cheek wet with dribble. You want them wake up so you could hear them say, "Bye, Daddy," but, same time, you scared they will. You *might* be able to bear it. Or you might just say, "Fuck

America," and stay.

In the stillness, you hear a engine purr and handbrakes jerk. Your brother-in-law, Declan, just pull up outside.

Judith with you by the kitchen table, going over everything one last time: ticket, departure card, Rufus address, virgin passport. You tuck them inside the same bomber jacket you did wear to the Embassy.

Your almost-empty suitcase standing up by the door—halfway in, halfway out—like it have two minds 'bout this whole thing. You and Judith hug and you kiss her on the cheek. Then, you put her at arm's length. Is time to go—Declan waiting—but the last seven years, they come like glue. Your palms not budging from the sleeve of Judith nightie.

You fake a grin and say, "Take care of them li'l fellas, eh."

And you linger, hoping she say something tender; so you could say something tender too. Something like *I frighten* or *I will miss you.*

But it don't happen. So you just leave Judith right there, leaning on the doorframe like she propping up the house.

October first, you touch down in JFK. The place big, big, big and bright, bright, bright. It come like you in one of them sci-fi movies where they land the plane inside a spaceship. Only shiny metal and white light.

Everybody else seem to know where they going so you fall in and follow the crowd. In the immigration line, your heart racing just like in the Embassy—like you guilty of something.

The officer asking almost the same questions and you give the same answers. He do so—Bam!—and stamp your passport for six months. *Hallelujah!*

You find your suitcase in no time—thanks to the orange ribbon Judith did tie on it. Then, the crowd take you past the customs desk and through a wall of doors that just open up by itself.

You in a big, wide clearing with metal barriers all 'round. Just beyond, it have at least three rows of faces and signs, plenty handmade signs. And plenty eyes aiming at you, but looking past you—you's not who they want. You freeze on the spot, like fuckin' stage fright. You trying to sift through, to find that one face, the only one you know in New York City. Seconds ticking and your spit drying out on your tongue like rain on the road. What if he forget?

"Junior! Yo, Junior! Over here!" Rufus find you. He a li'l way off to the side of the crowd waving, like he signaling a plane. "Welcome to the US of A!" he say, hugging you hard.

"Thanks, man. Thanks," you say.

Is a long, hot drive to Queens. Why the ass Rufus don't put on the air condition? But he saying is the last summer weather so enjoy it while you can.

The air different, kinda crispy. But you surprised how dull and dingy the place looking. Brown everywhere. And kinda factoryish—big, big chimney and pipe and lorry in the yard. A small hope start bleeping inside you—maybe you'll find MET work here; maybe this grocery thing is just a start.

Then, the streets get narrow and you reading signs:

check-cashing, car wash, Rite Aid, eyebrow threading. What the ass is eyebrow threading? And where all the damn white people? You thought New York streets would be crawling with them, but you only seeing brown faces, like yours.

Another right turn and is strictly houses now—all the same type but different colors. Rufus stop and get out to open a saggy chain link gate.

Rotting garbage sneaking up in your nose-hole. It have to be garbage. It can't be shit, right? This is America, for chrissake. Still, you don't say nothing to Rufus because you don't want to embarrass the man. You get your suitcase and follow him.

"But this is one big, *macco* house you have here, Rufus!"

"Yeah," he say, "Top-floor rented out to some Jamaicans. But I hooked you up, cuz. You got the whole basement to yourself."

The basement turn out to be some pipes and pillars, a rust-bitten washing machine and dryer, a plain cement floor. But in one corner, near the stairs, it have a crooked, wooden room leaning up on the concrete wall. As Rufus unlocking the door he grin just like your son Kevin and say, "Built this myself. Used to rent it to a Paki, but I threw him out for you."

It don't have much in the room. A patchy old couch (Rufus show you how to fold it out to a bed), a TV, another contraption he say is a electric heater, a closet and a musty smell. But say what: you in America! That's the only damn thing that matter.

Rufus say, "Look, I gotta bounce, kid. Shift starts at six. Take a nap or whatever. If you're hungry, help yourself to anything upstairs."

"I could call home?" you say.

Rufus open his wallet and flip a card in your direction.

Turning away, he say, "Just read the back and follow the instructions. Phone's in the kitchen. You're gonna have to stock up on that shit."

"First thing tomorrow," you say, running up the stairs behind him.

"And remember, the deal is . . ."

"Yeah, I know: basement free this first month; buy my own food; two hundred a month after that."

"A'ight," Rufus say. He point to the phone on the wall and duck out the side door.

Leg shaking, you dial; following the voice instructions, waiting for the international beep, praying you didn't mess up.

"Hello," Judith answer.

Boom! You could jump for joy.

"I reach," you say.

"Hello? Junior?"

"Yeah, is me. I reach."

"Junior? Hello?"

You shouting in the receiver but Judith still not hearing you.

Work at the grocery start bright and early the next day. It turn out not to be in the meat room. Ahmed, the manager, save that better-paying job for a fella from his own country, Palestine. You get the $4.25-a-hour job packing shelves and swiping goods with a li'l sticker-gun.

Becky is a cashier. The only white girl. She think she down with all the other cashiers but you hear them laughing behind her back and calling her "fat white trash."

That evening, you decide to buy some groceries. It late, the store ready to close. Becky is the only one still open. As you set down your things she say, "You don't talk much, do you, Island Man?"

You laugh.

"Ah! See, he smiles!" she say, and you smile a li'l wider. "So, you got a family back home?" she ask.

"Two boys."

"Lucky bastard. How old?"

"Seven and four."

"Miss 'em yet?"

You nod.

"Married?"

"Nah." Technically, is the truth. But a truth with plenty holes in it, like the netting on this paw-paw you buying. You smile in a guilty way. But Becky blushing, as if your smile have something to do with her. *Ha, Lord! This fat-girl think you desperate or what?*

She making small talk, punching in prices—mostly from memory. But then you notice she skipping over some things, just pushing them down the belt. You think is a mistake—she must be distracted with all the chit-chat—so you stretch out your hand to stop the next can. Becky watch you dead in the eye and wink.

You bag your groceries and burn road home.

You boil water and make some Top Ramen. Chili-Lime Shrimp. The thing smelling like fuckin' insecticide—tasting worse—but at least it warm. You eat on the edge of the sofa-bed, watching the TV, but really the damn thing watching you 'cause your mind so fuckin' far right now.

This is the first time you ever thief anything in life. Suppose Ahmed find out and call the police? Suppose they post your ass back to Trinidad? Imagine you: in a vest, short pants, and handcuffs, waddling off the plane; your boys ducking down 'cause they shame. You decide never to do this thing again—never, ever. And you decide to pay it back by working extra hard and doing anything the boss ask you to do. You will make yourself Ahmed li'l bitch.

And—*Shit!*—you keep that promise. You punch your card every day at seven and punch out every night at nine. Sometimes you doing double shifts. Sometimes you covering for people. Still, every red cent of your weekly salary spend-out before you even get it. It have Rufus rent to save up, Judith money to send, and you trying to full a barrel with food-and-thing to ship home for Christmas. A few groceries for yourself now and then—soup, bread, cheese—but, for a fella in your situation, phone cards is Life. America over-lonely. Just work, work, work, then this empty room. So you don't mind: you would rather starve than not hear your children.

Becky, she realize you don't take no lunch break. She ask 'bout it one day and you brush her off with a weak joke: you maintaining your physique. Couple days later—lunchtime self—you taking a smoke outside with Carlos, the Dominican fella from Produce.

"Ma-a-n," he say, "you peep that sexy new *morena* 'cross the street at the dry cleaners?"

"Nah, which one that is, boy?"

"Short. Thick. *Tremendo culo.*" He move his hands like he tracing a big, round pumpkin.

"Oh, she? Yeah, I glimpse her yesterday. But that's not my scene, brother."

"Whattaya mean, *amigo*? You don't see that ass?"

You laugh and explain, "I not really into fat girls, you know, Carlos. Gimme the smallies, the chicken-wings. You see how I *magga*? I like girls to suit my size. When a woman drop she leg on me in the night, I mustn't dead in my sleep."

Carlos slapping his thigh and dancing around. He swear you's the funniest man he ever meet. Chilling out like this, talking big—the way you does talk back home—and having somebody appreciate you for it. It real nice. A nice change from licking American ass whole day: *Yes, the brussel sprouts is right this way, ma'am . . . No, sir, don't worry, I'll clean that mess right up.*

A noise come from behind, inside the loading bay. You spin 'round; Becky standing up there clutching a li'l Ziploc bag with both hands.

Oh, fuck! Maybe she hear what you just say 'bout fat girls? Apart from Carlos, she's your only friend here. You don't want to hurt her feelings.

Becky just giggle, "Oops! Male-bonding," hand you the sandwich and walk off, back to her register. Each half of her bottom trembling to a different beat, like they suffering from two separate earthquakes.

You like Becky. She real easygoing. Always happy, always joking. When she laugh, she does make a noise like hiccups and her freckles does bounce like they in a Carnival band. But, you starting to get the vibes that Becky want you to *love* her.

She say she from Pennsylvania. Thirty-five, never married, no kids. She living with roommates, a bunch of other "ex-Amish girls" catching up on life. You don't know much 'bout Amish people except what you see on TV: they does pray plenty, farm plenty, and they don't like outsiders. *You* must be as outsider as it get, so you very surprised that Becky always squeezing in a line or two 'bout how *black men are so hot* and how *the Caribbean accent is so sexy.* Like is only one fuckin' accent for everybody in the whole Caribbean Sea. *Steups!*

One day, Becky come out plain, plain and ask, "So, you're not married, but is there . . . anyone? Special, I mean?"

You hear yourself say, "Special? Nah. Just my children-mother." And you almost expect a cock to crow because you feel like Judas Fuckin' Iscariot. You don't know why you keep doing this shit! Hiding Judith. But you just have this gut feeling things will go better for you, in America, if you hang a fuckin' sign 'round your neck: *Come in. I open . . . to everything.*

Rufus home on his off-night and y'all watching *Die Hard with a Vengeance* on his illegal pay-per-view. You tell him 'bout Becky. "My man!" he say. "That's your meal-ticket, yo!"

When you look confuse, he spell it out in neon. "Nigga, you better fuck that white heifer and get yourself straight. Yeah, they gave you six months. But you can flip that into a lifetime, with a green card."

Frowning, you wonder if you hear right. Rufus know Judith; he does stay by your house every Carnival; he's eat her food; and she does much-him-up. They kinda close. You start to wonder if Judith set him up to test you or something.

"The fuck you looking at me like that for?" Rufus say. "I ain't telling you fall in love with the bitch. I'm saying: make *her* love *you*. Opportunity's knocking and you need to respond, nigga. Think about your family."

You still gaping at Rufus like you no habla ingles. He shrug and done the talk, "People get married for papers all the time, cuz. This the US of A, remember."

Your mind sign off from Bruce Willis problems. You glimpsing now that you been thinking way too small 'bout yours. Why keep sending your family sandwich money when you could bring them to a fuckin' banquet?

Rufus damn right: being here in America ain't about your preference. What kinda girls you like or what kinda work you qualified for. Is about keeping yourself ready: knees bent, palms cupped. And juicing the fuck out of every opportunity that drop down.

Make Becky love you, Rufus did say. Make she love you till she would do anything to keep you. Sign on that dotted line, even. Yeah, you could do that. But you have to work quick—only five months left.

Later that night, you start feeling shaky 'bout your decision, so you call home.

Judith hear the beep and bawl, "Boys! Come quick! Is allyuh father." The connection real good this time: you actually hear their rubber slippers going plap, plap, plap. Some rustling; a couple thuds—they fighting for the phone. Jason win and Kevin start to cry. While Judith petting him, you ask Jason 'bout school, if he behaving himself.

"A boy did push li'l Kevin down in school," he say. "But I find the fella and push him back harder." He singing the whole story in his high-pitch voice.

"Good," you say, "stick up for him, eh. Always. You name Big Brother."

Then you talk to Kevin. He parrot everything his big brother just say, only with a lisp. As you listen, you close your eyes. Rufus right: is not about just feeding them. If you bring them to America you could give them what Luther Sr. and Janice never give you and Gail: a head start in life.

Then, Judith come on. She do a quick run-through: your mother and sister doing good, light bill and cable bill paid up, no water because the landlord didn't pay that bill, send the money Western Union next time (Moneygram line always too long).

She on top of everything. Super-capable. That's how it is with Judith. She don't neglect a single duty, but she does make you feel bad for making her do it—like you's not enough man. Before you fly-out, she did open her legs for you, but she never make a fuckin' sound. She hard.

Her voice change now, though—low and trembling—when she say, "It had another shooting. Right outside the school. The snow-cone vendor. They say he was a gang member."

"The boys see?" you ask, hoarse, because you frighten bad.

"Nah. They was in class, thank God. But still, Junior . . ."

"I know, I know."

Jason and Kevin. You could send them all the money in America; that can't block them from a Pleasantview bullet.

Winter coming fast. Your first. Your nose bleeding every time you step outside, your skin gray and itchy. You never been this fuckin' cold. And you miss your sons so bad it come like a toothache that does fill up your head and get worse and worse every day.

Soon, the bomber jacket not cutting it no more. Rufus lend you some stuff—coat, gloves, scarf, beanie—and you find some boots in the thrift store on Merrick Boulevard. Hand-me-downs, but fuck that! You stepping high these days, since Laparkan Shipping collect the barrel you was filling. Six weeks, they say—it'll get to Trinidad in time for Christmas.

Now, you have time, a li'l extra cash; now, you focusing on Becky.

Four and a half months to go.

You start lining up your day off with hers. Green Acres Mall every week. Is the closest thing to dating. But you's the illegal and she's the citizen, so she doing most of the spending: cologne, down jacket, Timberlands. Watch something too long and Becky buying it for you. Is a new feeling, a woman treating you so. It come like she's Mr. H and you's Gail. It too easy; you don't trust this set-up.

So, you never slack off. Is work, work, work. Through Thanksgiving, Christmas, New Years. But your day off, that's always for Becky.

One freezing Sunday in January, you bouncing towards the food court to get some General Tso's Chicken, when Becky say, "No. Let's eat next door, at the Ponderosa."

"That place look pricey," you say.

Becky wink. "Today's special. We've been friends now for exactly three months and five days. It's like . . . our anniversary or something."

Becky grab your hand, pull you through the mall and across the street, to the all-you-can-eat restaurant. You real excited. They don't have nothing like that back home.

Becky taking a bit of this, a bit of that; li'l ants' nests of food—plenty less than you woulda expect for her size. But you! You make a fuckin' mountain.

Back in the booth, she snuggle up—close, close—while you shovel food in your mouth.

"I was thinking," she say, pick-picking at her plate, "you could show me your place today. It's near, right?"

Like a dumb-ass, you blink a few times. You didn't plan on making The Move today. You was easing up to it, thinking you needed a few more weeks. Then she woulda be ready to give you the punani. Nah, that's a lie. You was stalling 'cause *you* not ready. To horn Judith for the first time. To sex Becky when you ain't even attracted to her. And not just sex her—no—you have to *fuck* her, till she seeing stars and you getting stripes. Till she love you and want to keep you in America.

Rufus in your head: opportunity knocking, boy. Respond.

Fifteen minutes later, you and Becky on the bus heading to your place.

Rufus cooking pelau and blasting old-time calypso. When you introduce Becky he switch on the Trini charm: kiss-up her hand, bear-hug like they's old friends. She blush and then "Feeling Hot, Hot, Hot" come on. She bawl, "Oh my God, I love this song!" and start doing a totally outta-time, white-girl conga while she sing, "Olé, Olé! Olé, Olé!" You and Rufus clap but you feeling shame for Becky. As you turn away and start leading her downstairs to the basement, Rufus slap you twice on the back.

You turn on the TV; it have nowhere to sit but the bed. It creaking; will the li'l fold-out legs take you plus Becky? You not even sure how to do this: you may be a liar but your prick ain't; it does always tell the truth.

She say, "Brrrr! It's chilly down here," and latch on to your side.

You lower your lashes, like you drawing the drapes, and give her a cock-lip smile. You make your voice velvet as you say, "Lemme warm you up."

You put a arm 'round Becky, kiss her. Soft, lips-only, shy. You still listening for some reaction from your prick. Radio fuckin' silence.

Her kiss getting aggressive, she treating your face like chocolate. Still nothing. She dip down suddenly and squeeze your crotch. Still spongy.

Then Becky push you backwards on the bed. The springs creak again as she wriggle off to kneel on the floor. When her lips wrap you up, a sigh leak through your teeth. You don't have to worry again. In fact, you don't have to do nothing but lie there, staring at the beams-and-them. Becky using her tongue like a magic wand. You don't know where she pull out a rubbers from, but she rolling it on for you. Then she climb on. Slow. And you feel like you's Moses rod and she's the Red Sea. "Oh Gawwwd," you moan. If this was Judith you woulda look— spread them knees and look, play with it li'l bit. But now, you squeeze your eyes tight, tight and wrap your hand in the sheet. You concentrate on the feeling. Not the person. And you tune in your ears to all the cussin' and groanin' and all the claims that you's the biggest she ever had and she think she gonna tear and she in so much pain but it feeling so good to her. And the American accent. Man, you fucking a white chick! With your eyes closed this could be any white chick: Carmen Electra, Anna Nicole Smith—any-damn-body you want it to be.

You and Becky been at it for weeks.

You still sending money for Judith, you still calling. You filling a second barrel—Becky helping.

It come like you have two lives, two parallel tracks that never cross. You keep hopping lanes but nobody noticing and everybody happy like pappy.

Still, time ticking down. Rufus say you ain't staying in the basement even one day past six months. "I ain't harboring no illegal," he say. "For INS to come kick down my fuckin' door? Nuh-uh, nigga! I done told you: get that bitch married, or get her pregnant. Or go the fuck home."

Something have to happen soon. The tricky part, the part you spend whole nights studying, is how to mention marriage to Becky without looking like a asshole.

One day, she find you in the aisle, labeling cereal boxes. She giggling so much she resemble the Jell-O heap by Ponderosa. She say she get a letter from her cousin, Naomi, down in Florida—a next ex-Amish chick. Naomi getting married—finally!—in June. Becky want you go to the wedding.

Like a fuckin' marksman, you see the shot and take it. "I can't, babes. Remember, my visa up April 1?" You know she don't "remember" 'cause you never said it before.

"This April? Oh my God! That's two months away," Becky say. Her hands fly up like two frighten doves. They rest on her mouth.

She back away from you a few feet, then turn and speed off. She glum and quiet, quiet whole day—nothing you say or do is funny.

Late that night, you in the basement, watching Knight Rider reruns. Guiltiness resting, like a concrete block, on your conscience. You toying with the idea of calling Trinidad. You need to hear Judith voice; to make sure that the home-fires still burning, that if all else fail you still have her and the boys. You never once, ever cheat on her. This thing you trying with Becky shouldn't count neither. Yes, you was unfaithful, but it have a bigger picture: you was fucking for betterment. For the whole family.

Somebody knock the basement door just as the line in Trinidad start ringing. "Vis-i-tor!" The way Rufus say it, you know is Becky.

You barely hang up the phone before she walk in and slam the door. Face on fire. Huffing and puffing. She might blow the whole damn house down.

"So that's it? That was your plan? Fuck the fat girl for a few months, then leave? Go back to the island? To your kids' mom? Your wife? Or whatever. I don't even know."

"You have it all wrong," you say. "I tell you: she and me, we done, babes. That's why I in America. Look, I know you mad that I never say I leaving so soon. But, to be honest, I was hoping something woulda work out by now, so I wouldn't have to go. I talk to Ahmed 'bout work permit—but he ain't biting. It have some chick by Rufus job who willing to get married, but we gotta pay her, like, six thousand or something. I ain't got that."

You doing good so far. Only one lie: about Judith.

Becky stop shifting from side to side. She listening now, believing—you hope.

"C'mere," you say, in your new yankee twang, as you slide to the edge. When she sit down, you hold her hands and say, "Babes, I wouldn't play you. It hurting me that you thinking so. This here between us—this shit is real, yo. And I want it get realer. But I'mma run out of options soon. I don't wanna be one of those guys, like Carlos, who overstay and then gotta spend his whole life dodging cops."

"But you wouldn't have that problem if you stayed," Becky say.

"How you figure that?" you ask, faking dumb.

"*We* could get married."

Boom! But still, you draw back and say, "Naw, babes I couldn't ask you to . . ."

"No, I want to. And you wouldn't have to pay me or anything. 'Cause like you said, this shit is real and we're heading there anyway. Right? This'll just be a li'l sooner."

"Right," you say, "but I never want you to feel I using you 'cause . . ."

"I know you're not," Becky say, resting her finger on your lips. "Otherwise, you wouldn't have taken the time . . . been such a gentleman . . . with me."

You shrug and look bashful.

"So, Luther Archibald Junior, will you marry me?"

As you say yes, your pores and your cock raise the same time. Adrenaline. But you don't know if is fright or excitement.

You fuck, and afterward you go up in the kitchen together and make scramble eggs. Becky spend the whole night this time. Y'all barely fit on the sofa-bed but is okay; you don't do much sleeping anyway. Becky talk and talk, 'bout the wedding, the future. You listen and nod, in a daze almost. You keep seeing Jason face: Christmas morning, two years back, when he rip off the gift-paper and see the remote-control tractor he did wish for; and how he start to cry when you drive it and blow the horn—because it get too real, too sudden.

By morning, though, everything settle; you and Becky raise a new plan, shiny like a foil balloon.

You not going home April 1. You and Becky getting married in March—a few weeks away. You'll get a apartment together. You'll go to a immigration lawyer—it have one in the strip-mall across from the supermarket. Your papers should come through in two, three years. A year or so again for the boys' papers. By that time, you'll have a better job, a nicer place to live. They'll come across.

Becky, she super-excited. She getting a new, readymade family for the old one in Pennsylvania that cut her off.

"I'll love those boys like my own," she say.

You won't actually need her by then, but it nice to hear Becky thinking so.

And it have a next part to the plan you don't tell her. After they come across, the boys will file for their mother. You will make sure it happen. Until then, you'll send money for Judith every month and she will never, ever want for nothing as long as you alive. She might be cold, she might be hard, she might not love you—but she's your children-mother.

***

Sunday, you call home as usual. You tell Judith: Ahmed sponsoring the green card. METs in short, short supply in New York. With all the old machinery in the S-Town Supermarket chain, they need a man with your skills.

Judith voice get high and girlish as she bawl, "Oh God, for true, Luther?"

"Is not a now-for-now thing," you warn. "And it mean I can't come home in April, maybe not for years. Not until they organize the papers and the lawyer give the green light."

"That's okay," she quick to say. "We'll manage. Ain't we managing now? And the li'l sacrifice is for the boys. So I don't mind. Do what you have to do, Luther."

Humph! Something drop in your belly and drag. You glad Judith making this so easy but, same time, you wishing she struggle—just a li'l bit—with not seeing you for so long. She sounding like you and she been simple business partners this whole time—and the boys is the business.

Then Judith ask, "So after your papers go in, how long before we could get married?"

Your blood turn icy-slush in your veins.

"Ain't we have to be man-and-wife for you to file for me? Besides, you don't think is time? Seven years, remember?"

"W'happen, girl? Like you feel I go leave you out or what? I can't believe you thinking so low, Judy."

She back down. For now.

March 16, ten days before your City Hall wedding, you in work swiping can beets and trying to decide what color waistband to get with the tuxedo Becky renting. Ahmed peep out his office and shout down the lane, "Lu-ta! Phone call!"

"Me?" you bawl, jumping up from the stool and dropping the pricing gun. On impact, the thing split in half—you'll have to glue it together again, for the third time.

"Yes, you, mu-tha-foo-ka."

Ahmed watching you hard, hard. He barely move out the doorway to let you in.

Breathless, you say, "Hello?"

Then, the nicotine croak: Janice. "Junior? Is you, son?"

"Yes, Mammy. Is me." Your mind gone straight to Judith and the boys. *Oh God, another shooting by the school!*

Janice start crying and you can't make out a word. Judith come on. The boys fine, she say.

"So why allyuh calling me here? I can't talk."

"Listen, you have to come home. Police lock up Gail. And Janice, like she going crazy here."

"What?" you say, a li'l too loud. Ahmed step back in the office. But God help him if he try take this phone out your hand now!

"Yeah, they say she shoot the old man," Judith explain.

"Mr. H? What happen?"

"The story still hazy. But it look like she was pregnant and she find him with a next woman. He beat she and she loss the child. She did move back in by Janice last week. Then, next thing we know—*Pow!*—she shoot the man."

"Fuck!"

You walk back to your stool but you don't sit. You just stand up there, middle of the canned foods aisle, staring down at the pricing gun—how it skin-open on the floor, orange stickers spilling out like guts.

You, is you to blame, Luther.

You shoulda do what you really wanted to do when you first hear 'bout Gail and Mr. H. You shoulda walk up in his cloth-store, ask to see him in his office, close the door, lean over his desk, point in his face, and threaten his Syrian ass. You shoulda warn him that Gail not alone in this world, that she have a big brother. A brother who know every Pleasantview backstreet inside out, who have friends in Lost Boyz gang, Red Kings gang, and other low places. And that he need to get the fuck outta Gail life.

But then, how she woulda eat? You wasn't helping.

Okay. Then why you never talk to Gail sheself? Why you never tell her what you, as a man, know 'bout men like Mr. H? That he was planning to suck her dry like a plum seed, then move on to the next ripe one. Why you never warn her? That when you fucking for betterment is okay to let them keep you, but you must never let them own you. Control your damn feelings. And don't plan no long future with them—get what you need and get out.

But no, you didn't do none of that. Ain't, Luther?

You pick up the pricing gun and re-roll the tape. With some slapping and squeezing, you reattach the two halves. A few practice clicks and it working again. You crouch to the bottom shelf and start shooting cans, shooting fast.

Fast like how your heart beating.

Fast like how you thinking.

What if it was one of your boys in this mess? What if it was li'l Kevin in trouble, and Jason didn't show up? Or the other way around?

Nah, that's not how you raising them, Luther. They does stick together.

Well, they getting older, smarter. What if you don't go back for Gail, and one day those same boys watch you and say, "Why, Daddy? Ain't you's she big brother?"

Half hour pass. You done price-out everything.

You slide off the stool, to the cold floor. Arms across knees, you make a hammock for your head—it heavy. With your own disappointment. And, you steeling yourself to tell Becky that your sister get lock-up and you have to go home tomorrow. And if you survive that, you have to gear up to comfort your mother, to meet Gail lawyer, to walk in the jail. You excited to see the boys again but you 'fraid to see Judith, to lie next to her, lie to her face.

Judith and Becky. Becky and Judith. You been feeding them so much stories: candy soak in cocaine—they eating out your hands, licking your sticky palms, begging for more. Now, you got to keep everything straight in your head, Luther—at least for the next thirty days—till you make it back to America, till they stamp you for a next six months. Is a rare thing: two back-to-back stamps. But you been lucky so far. Don't be lucky and coward, Luther. Go brave. If you could do that, nobody getting hurt; everybody staying hopeful. Even you.

Santimanitay[2]

THE OFFICIAL WAKE FOR MR. H was scheduled for tonight, up the mountain, on the grounds of his mansion, Elysium. It was by invitation only. Miss Ivy hadn't received one and she felt like a chupidee because she'd expected otherwise—those people owed her, for chrissake.

Flat on her bed, she studied the continental stains across her fifty-something-year-old fiberboard ceiling. She wanted to pee, but her neighbor, Winston, was in the toilet they shared. He was singing a Frank Sinatra song, "I Did It My Way." Had she been feeling better, she would've already marched into the corridor to bang on the door and say, "Winston, hush your mouth and open your ass quicker! People waiting."

In fact, had she been well, she would've put on her better funeral dress and her fur coat—the same one Joan—the great Mrs. H—had passed along as a retirement gift—and Miss Ivy would've travelled up to Elysium. Invitation or no invitation,

---

2. A traditional refrain to each verse of an *extempo* war. Derived from the French, "sans humanité", which is loosely translated as "without mercy." Extempo is a calypso artform where verses are made up on the spot, in response to a particular stimulus or challenge, usually in a lyrical war between two or more calypsonians.

she would've gone. But, since the night when that young girl, Gail, shot Mr. H, Miss Ivy had been unwell. She'd felt herself succumbing to a weakness that had teeth and tongue and a long, empty belly. At first, thinking it was a case of maljo, she'd tried all the usual cures for bad-eye—saying prayers, bathing with blue laundry soap, pinning blue cloth to her bosom—but nothing had helped. This evening, she'd started hurting here and there, all over. And now, she wished she could just lie still, die quick and leave this blasted life.

Winston started from the top, again. Miss Ivy sucked her teeth, eased up and planted her swollen feet on the floor. From below the bed, she dragged her blue enamel posey. The way it scraped the floorboards, she could tell: under there needed a good sweeping. She hadn't been able with all that bending lately. It made her dizzy in a way she hadn't experienced since that vomit-stink boat trip from Grenada to Trinidad when she was twelve years old.

She squatted over the posey, began to pee, and the release seemed to make things clear. It's not that she wanted to rub shoulders with the businessman friends and political croneys of Mr. H. No, she would've felt too ashamed to act like she was their equal. Instead, she would've stayed in the kitchen, helping the caterers or something. She might've even remained after the guests left, to help clean up. Depending on Joan's mood, Miss Ivy might've even spent the night at Elysium—maybe even a few days—to make sure Joan was sleeping and eating properly, instead of chugging coffee, Scotch and Valium. After twenty years of service in that household, Miss Ivy knew that was how Joan coped with stress. Humph! You could cook rich people's food, clean their shitty toilets, bend over backward, and keep their dirty secrets for twenty-something years but, when one of them dies, suddenly you're not good enough to mourn with them.

That's why no invitation had come.

Fine, fine, Miss Ivy thought, reaching for the toilet paper inside her bedside table—the door had fallen off since the days when the table belonged to Mr. H's daughter. Let them big-shots stay up there with their hors d'oeuvres and posh, sippy-sippy drinks.

A *real* wake for Mr. H was happening right now, right here in Pleasantview. No invitation was necessary—anybody could come. Plenty Pleasantview people had worked for Mr. H, so this was *the people's* wake, to prove the small-man knew how to grieve for the biggest big-shot in the village. *We have our own ways to cope,* Miss Ivy assured herself. That was probably why Winston was singing that song: he was practicing for tonight. He'd been a popular calypsonian in his day—The Mighty Raven was his soubriquet—and he'd even toured America and met Harry Belafonte . . . or so he claimed. Winston liked to think he was the official minstrel of Pleasantview wakes, and he always got offended when other calypsonians showed up. Miss Ivy hoped none would tonight; she wanted a peaceful, quiet wake. Feeling as kilkitay as she was, she couldn't handle too much confusion and wele-wele tonight.

She planted one hand on the table, hoisted herself and hobbled to the side of the room she called her kitchen. She gripped the burglar bars, stretching onto tiptoes to unlatch the window so she could macco next door, into the rumshop yard where the wake had already started. A good-sized crowd. And two tables with four men each. Miss Ivy knew those fellas must be itching to return to their All Fours card game. But, they sat with bowed heads as Sister Yolande from the Pentecostal Church led the crowd in prayers. The wind brought the loud beginnings of her sentences: Father Jesus . . . And Father Jesus . . . Yes, Father Jesus.

Miss Ivy limped to the other window and, from her room, she looked across the few feet of patchy grass, weeds and dog shit, at the blue kitchen door of the apartment where Gail used to live. In the dark, with only borrowed and reflected light, the door seemed to be floating. It gave Miss Ivy a spooky feeling. A young girl like that, so mashed-up by a man that she could point a gun and pull a trigger. As if retracing Gail's steps, Miss Ivy's eyes moved to the couch where Gail had sat just a few weeks ago, confessed she was "making child for Mr. H", begged Miss Ivy to "read the cards to see if he go leave he wife". Miss Ivy had tried to counsel the girl: *You only nineteen, don't bet your life on that man and his stinking lies.* But Gail had been so stubborn— she'd thought she was special to Mr. H—and she'd even accused Miss Ivy of being jealous: "You did fuck him too, ain't?" she'd said.

In truth, Miss Ivy hadn't wanted to see Gail find happily- ever-after. It had seemed unfair that, after only one year, Gail should be rewarded, when, for almost twenty years, Miss Ivy had endured that man's clammy hands and gotten nothing for it—except a hand-me-down fur coat. Was that jealousy? Had it stopped her from doing and saying more to help Gail? Miss Ivy had asked herself these questions every night since the shooting. This whole thing was a downright weeping shame: Mr. H in a casket, Gail in jail. That's why it didn't matter how sick she felt, Miss Ivy *had* to go to a wake—any wake— tonight. With the things she'd seen and the things she knew, she was the only person who could truly mourn for them: two lives lost just so . . . no, three . . . she counted the baby, too.

Winston had stopped singing. She slipped the fur coat over her dress and banged on the paneling between their rooms.

"Winston!"

"Oye!"

"You going wake?"

"Yeah, I leavin' now."

"Wait for me. I comin'."

Just as she turned the doorknob, another pain gripped Miss Ivy. Belly or chest—she couldn't tell. The ache climbed her left side with the casual pace of an iguana in a zaboca tree. She braced against the wall and waited. Maybe she should stay home? No, she needed to go, she needed to do her duty, she couldn't leave even a toe space for spiritual wickedness to step in. Her mother, a frequent wake-goer, had taught her that: *My pet, you must go no matter you love them or not. Go and release them, make them could travel in peace. Otherwise, they spirit coming back every night, to pull your toe and beg your pardon.* Miss Ivy didn't want Mr. H's spirit anywhere near her bedside at night. She took a few deep breaths and moved into the corridor. She was The Mighty Miss Ivy, Pleasantview's seer-woman, Mother Superior of the whole village, no kiss-meh-ass pain was going to keep her back tonight.

Winston stood in a dark suit and fedora hat, holding a guitar case, a bottle tucked in his armpit. Under the forty-watt bulb he was a young, dapper version of himself. "W'happen, girl?" he said, as Miss Ivy took a crooked step toward him. "You still feelin' sick?"

With the arm holding the guitar case, he offered his elbow. She took it, the camphor ball smell of his clothes coming as a welcome revival to her senses. "Is just a gas pain," she said, afraid to admit, out loud at least, that it was her heart hurting.

"All you need is a sip of this babash, girl," Winston said, waving the bottle. "My cousin-and-them make this down Moruga. It go burn out any problem you have inside you."

A young man gave Miss Ivy his seat. "Thank you, son," she said, raising her palm in that saintly gesture she'd seen in religious photographs—people expected these things from her. The young man bowed and backed away.

She drew the fur closer around her body. Sister Yolande, who sat behind, asked, "Ivy, why you don't take off that thing? Look how you sweating." Miss Ivy could've explained that she'd been cold-sweating all night, that her chest felt heavy and her intestine was a knotty shoelace. But she would've rather died than seem fragile to these people; they still believed in her "supernatural" powers.

"Yolande, mind your damn business," she said, mopping her face and neck with a rag.

One by one, folks passed and touched Miss Ivy's shoulder, the braver among them asking things like, "How you coping, doux-doux? You alright?" as if *she* were Mr. H's widow. Pleasantview people had more respect for her long service to that family than the damn family itself, it seemed.

As the gripe got worse and worse, Miss Ivy watched the All Fours players without really seeing them, except whenever a team exploded with "Hang Jack!" She mostly cocked her ears and tried to listen to the hushed-tone conversations around her . . . *They lie: she didn't shoot him, she stab him . . . She go get-off because the lawyer pleading insanity . . . He daughter—the lesbian one—she move back home.* Then, Miss Ivy heard something that spliced a different kind of pain through her body: *Why you think Ivy here and not in the wake up-the-road? Miss Joan don't want she by the house. Ivy did see the whole thing in the cards and she never warn Mr. H 'bout Gail.*

On any other night, Miss Ivy might have spun in the direction of the voice, and laced into the speaker like the Roman whip that beat Christ: *Look, haul yuh ass! What you know 'bout me and Miss Joan?* Tonight, though, Miss Ivy couldn't summon the strength for a fight. They were correct: Joan blamed her— not for Mr. H's death—but for other things, unspoken things. Miss Ivy had suffered for twenty years under Joan's cloaked-up rage: "You need to do better, Ivy . . . That window is spotty; wipe it over . . . This floor, don't use the mop, use the scrubbing brush and get on your knees—I know you're accustomed." And Joan had always behaved like it was Miss Ivy's fault Mr. H couldn't keep his hands to himself: "You need to dress more appropriately for work, Ivy . . . I don't want to see your panty-line, Ivy . . . Walking through my house, shaking your ass like that? Are you looking for attention, Ivy?" But Miss Ivy had needed her job, and Joan had needed her to hold the house together, so they'd become false friends and close enemies for twenty-something years. And for every one of those years, Joan had said, "Good help is hard to find, Ivy," when she'd handed over the Christmas bonus. Miss Ivy had always known "good help" meant "silence".

She shook her head now, recalling how many times she'd swallowed shame and forgiven Joan, but Joan had never forgiven *her* for Mr. H's sins. She might have, if she'd been there to see Miss Ivy fight: like that time he'd threatened to push her head deeper in the toilet-bowl if she didn't open her legs; that other time she'd been at the kitchen sink, chipping ice for one of the girls' birthday party, she'd pointed the ice pick and he'd prised it away, threatening to rake it across her face. "I will say I catch you thiefing," he'd said. "Who you think everybody will believe? Me or you?"

A big Crix tin appeared in front of Miss Ivy's face. Thinking the dryness of the cracker might help soak up the roiling bile in her stomach, she withdrew a trembling handful, and crunched as loud as she could—to block out the voices and the hissing shame. Somebody else offered coffee from a thermos but Miss Ivy knew better than to drink wake coffee—sugarless and deadly like black disinfectant.

From her bag, she pulled her own little canister. She held it at arm's length to avoid spillage, unscrewed the cap and fanned steam away. Ginger tea with cinnamon and honey, her mother's homemade recipe for bad-stomach. Miss Ivy brought the thermos to her mouth and closed her eyes over the first sip. She was no longer in Pleasantview, or even in Trinidad. She was on another island altogether: Grenada, in the kitchen of the tiny estate house, watching Mammy at the two-burner stove.

Gnarled black hands, knuckles swollen, grating ginger root, then splintering cinnamon bark, then boiling it all together. The tiny house engulfed in spicy aromas.

Miss Ivy felt the peace she'd only known back then, the peace of a common-fowl chick sitting in the coob, under its mother-hen's wing. *You does see your mother before you dead.* Miss Ivy hoped that old saying was true, because she hadn't seen Mammy since she'd left her in Trinidad, at twelve years old.

At Winston's voice, "Of course, I go sing," she opened her eyes and was back in the rumshop yard.

Winston sat on a chair facing the crowd, his back to the All Fours tables. He removed his fedora and rested it on the chair next to him. Under the street lamp, his bald head shone like a dog's balls in moonlight. Miss Ivy guessed that's what he wanted: to be seen, not in shadow, as he delivered the song he'd been practicing in the toilet.

She was surprised when, instead of Sinatra, Winston began strumming the familiar local chords of an extempo. "Help me," he encouraged the crowd, and they joined in, clapping and singing:

Pa–da–da da ta–da ta–da ta . . .
Is a real shame and a tragedy,
What happened in this small com–mu–nity.
Sad to see: a big businessman,
Get tie–up with that tricky young woman.
Although she know the man was married,
She push–up to make a baby for he.
When she couldn't get he money as she did plan,
She abort, then shoot the innocent man.

"Santimanitay!" the crowd sang, to end the verse. Then everybody laughed and applauded Winston.

Not Miss Ivy. She sat dead-faced, staring at him, but he wouldn't meet her gaze.

Winston knew what an ugly betrayal that verse was. He knew it hadn't been an abortion, but rather a beating from Mr. H that had started the bloodshed. She and Winston had been the only people there when Gail had thrown open her blue back-door and bawled for help. Miss Ivy had gotten to her first and found Gail on the floor, her dress pink everywhere but red between her legs where she had it balled-up and pressed down like a drain stopper.

"Father-Jesus! You try to kill the child yourself?" Miss Ivy had said, grabbing a kitchen towel. And when Gail said, "No, he beat me," Miss Ivy had offered the best lie she could, "Don't worry, sometimes they could still save it."

Winston had shown up and by the time they got Gail into the back seat of his car, the towel was soaked and blood was everywhere: on the upholstery, the glass, Miss Ivy's housedress. Even on Winston's hands. Those same hands still strumming the guitar, they had been shaking as he backed the vehicle out of the yard that evening.

How could Winston make a mockery of all that? For what? A few claps?

One of the All Fours players sprang up. Holding a half-empty rum bottle like a microphone, he moved toward Winston's chair, singing, "Pa-da-da da ta-da ta-da ta," in a voice that could grate cassava. When he pointed at the card-players and ordered,

"Play the tune!" they began a rhythmic pounding of the tables and the upside-down buckets on which they sat.

Winston plucked the guitar. He had no choice, with the crowd clapping and chanting the extempo lavway: *Pa-da-da da . . .* Miss Ivy could see, though, his flat smile peeling at the edges, like print on a cheap jersey. Winston hadn't expected an extempo battle, he hadn't expected anyone—especially a nobody, non-calypsonian—to challenge his lyrical mastery. *Yes, Lord,* she prayed, *let Winston punish.* Let this All Fours player put him to shame, with serious lyrics to make people think and weep out their liver-string tonight.

> *What you say just now, that is not true,*
> *So the facts I came to reveal to you.*
> *Old-man minding girl and he showing off,*
> *But in the bedroom he was really soft.*
> *So she pick-up with me who young, fit and quick,*
> *And she fall in love with my sugar-stick.*
> *I say I didn't want she with no other one,*
> *That's why: she get rid of the old man.*

"Santimanitay!" the crowd screamed, and the wake came alive then. People hooting, slapping their thighs and their neighbors' backs. People inside the rumshop running out to join the gleeful melée. This fella had taken the mauvais langue even further than Winston; he'd suggested Gail had killed for better sex. Pleasantview liked nothing better than a good bacchanal!

Miss Ivy laughed, too, but at the disappointment on Winston's face, and she found herself trembling with a kind of false excitement she recognized as panic. Like the first time with

Mr. H, him riding her on the bed she'd been trying to make, he'd turned on the vacuum and she'd let its screams be hers as, in her head, hooves pounded and animals grunted. Her eyes had been on the door, but she'd been seeing something else: her ten-year-old self in the stables of the Estate with that groom—the one who'd been bringing her peanut-candy for weeks and promising a horse ride. "Two more guava season and you go be ripe," he'd said, cupping his hands to measure her bee-sting breasts before sucking them. He'd helped her mount the new horse, Paraclete, then jumped up behind and yelled "Ya!" and the faster the horse went, the faster he'd made it go, until she'd thought she would fall off, she'd thought she would be trampled and die that way . . . under the horse or under the groom.

She must have groaned.

"You alright, Ivy?" Sister Yolande said, leaning over the chair between them as the noise died down. "Watch how your eye red and your face wet. Like you well laugh?"

Miss Ivy answered, "Girl, if you can't laugh, you go cry in this life, oui. Hear the wotless-man-and-them pouring shame like oil on the li'l girl head. Black and poor and plus a woman— that's the recipe for shame self." Miss Ivy raised her voice then, "Father Lord, forgive these jackasses!" she said.

A few murmuring heads turned with amused looks, then turned away.

"You don't study them," Yolande said, patting Miss Ivy's shoulder. "I go put these fellas in they place!" Then she hurried off, to the clearing where Winston still sat with his guitar. "Pa-da-da da ta-da ta-da ta," Yolande began, gospel choir reverberation in her voice. She did a two-step calypso dance to make her ass a swinging pendulum in Winston's face.

Miss Ivy stood, easing the sweaty, heavy fur from her shoulders, as she clutched the chair in front of her. She wanted to see and hear Yolande better. And she needed to do something with her body, something different. She was a tired, old rag who'd spent years sitting in dirty water. How many card-readings had she pretended to do—for old women, young women—and always about a vicious man or a lost child? Too many times she'd lied to give Pleasantview women false hope, to feel like she was helping them. But nothing had ever changed—in her life or theirs. Miss Ivy felt tattered, oversoaked and renk with secret female blood. She was dying to wring herself clean.

Yolande pointed a red-nailed, accusing finger at Winston and she sang:

> *Dog does run down puss, when dog feel to play.*
> *Then turn around and bawl the puss is to blame.*
> *How much young girl that old man hold down?*
> *And allyuh never talk 'cause he money strong.*
> *One baby dead, but it have plenty more.*
> *Fu-ne-ral, they bound to show up by Miss Joan door.*
> *Yes two bullet land, but three bullet miss.*
> *Gail shoulda cas-trate the son-offa-bitch.*

"Santimanitay!" the crowd roared. They were all on their feet now, over Miss Ivy, their silhouettes towering and clustering around her like a black forest. Winston strumming, the bucket brigade beating, the bottle-and-spoon man knocking *lik-ki-ting-lik-ki-ting-lik-ki-ting*—everybody on a faster rhythm now, faster than any extempo, and growing more frenetic with every second. They had started this night pretending to honor Mr. H's life and mourn his death. But Miss Ivy felt the ground trembling now, under the weight of a spiteful honesty descending on the rumshop like a chariot: Pleasantview was damn glad Mr. H dead! He had dishonored so many of them in life. He'd bought and discarded women, made men feel helpless and small. He was a son-offa-bitch and Yolande had given everybody license to say so.

In the press of bodies, Miss Ivy felt herself being carried away, swaying back and forth, unsteady on her feet. Just as she had been on the deck of the rusted ferry listing its way from Grenada to Trinidad, her neck craned as far over the rail as possible, waiting for the next spasm of vomit, a towel tucked over her blue dress. Mammy's voice rolling in and out upon the waves, "Weeping endure for the night, m'child. But joy cometh in the morning. Yuh belly still small, we go fix it. Stop cryin' and lef' that nasty stable-boy from your thoughts. You damn lucky Auntie keepin' you in Trinidad!"

The pain returned. Worse than ever, it clamped Miss Ivy's chest and back, keeping her upright and in place for more punishment. She shut her eyes and held tighter to the chair. Something was surfacing inside—being squeezed up from a long way down. She wanted it to come out. She made up her mind to wait for it and to bear the terrible, terrible squeezing pain. Sweat leaked like a briny hemorrhage from her open pores.

A new lavway started in the crowd. All Fours Player croaking, "Doh answer the telephone, Joan!" and the crowd responding, "Doh answer the telephone!" Back and forth the chant went, "Doh answer the telephone, Joan! . . . Doh answer the telephone!" Still, Miss Ivy waited. Bongo drums appeared from God-knows-where, bongo dancing began, bodies flailing under the flickering streetlight . . . *lik-ki-ting-lik-ki-ting-lik-ki-ting* . . . still, Miss Ivy waited.

At last, her throat constricted and her mouth fell open. She groped for someone, anyone, and a young woman reeled and reached out.

With eyes wide and unseeing, Miss Ivy whispered to her, "He rape me," then, as if a cork had left a bottle, there came a loud rush of words, "Allyuh, he used to rape me! He was a raper-man!"

The drumming stopped, the wake fell silent.

Everybody in the rumshop yard heard when Miss Ivy cried out, "Satan, receive your son! You's my onliest hope now!" Then the vomit flowed, she collapsed over the chair, as over the rim of a boat and, while tumbling toward those imagined waters, her mind clung tight to a thread of blue . . . .

The blue hundred-dollar notes inside the envelope Gail had sent her to retrieve from the bedroom, to pay the hospital; the blue notes Joan had given her for twenty-something years of salary and Christmas bonus and fortune-telling and secret-keeping . . . blue, as the shirt Mr. H had on when she'd walked into his study and told him about the blisters and the burning and how she must've gotten it from him, and the blue blocks of laundry-soap she'd bathed with every time the blisters returned . . . the blue pieces of cloth she'd always pinned to other people's children to protect them from maljo and the jealous spirits of unborn babies, all the while thinking of her own . . . . The blue blanket on the floor of the stable and the bluish eye of the horse-fly squatting on it, studying her, and when she'd turned her head away to stare over the stable-boy's shoulder and between the flapping galvanize sheets, the crisp Grenada sky . . . the chipped blue paint on a pirogue in Gouyave bay, its net paid out, and the darker blue of the troubled waters as men frightened fish and herded them forward, while other men with blue-black glistening skin stood on the shore pulling seine, pulling together to bring in the net, pulling to a rhythm, pulling to the excited voices of children on the beach. Ivy was there, again, among those picky-head children, some with plaits still tight, some with plaits loosed and hair exploding, all black and barebacked and all in underwear, hers a blue panty—they hadn't yet learned that boys and girls were different, and she hadn't yet learned how to feel ashamed.

Epilogue: Kings of the Earth

JASON WAKE UP EARLY O'CLOCK, BUT he didn't come off the bed because it woulda look too fishy, especially on a Monday. He had a secret plan this morning, a kinda Mission Impossible thing, starting from the parlour on Watts Trace, then to the Muslim man waiting behind the masjid. Jason lie down there, a li'l nervous, rehearsing what he had to do and say, until (finally!) his mother, Judith, pound the bedroom door and bawl, "Boys, time to get cracking." Jason slide off the top bunk and start tickling Kevin, his li'l brother, foot.

"Hurry up, Small Man. I busy this morning," Jason say.

Kevin groan and turn, but didn't wake up. When Jason tickle his belly, Kevin whole body was hot, hot.

"W'happen, Kev? You okay?" Jason say.

"I not feelin' good," Kevin groan. "Where Mammy?"

Jason run in the kitchen for Judith.

"Oh God, don't tell me this child sick again," she say, and she stop pasting corn beef on bread. She jab the knife at Jason and say, "I never had so much trouble with you, but this next one . . . he like a egg."

"He can't help it, Mammy."

"I know. But is me alone." She slam down the knife, and

204

corn beef splatter. "Doctor bill—is me. Pharmacy—is me. I done use up all my holidays behind this boy, I can't stay home again." Judith chest was moving fast, fast—up and down—like a cry trying to buss out and she trying to trap it inside.

Jason watch his mother and feel so sorry for her.

"Your father was sickly just so, you know. Same bronchitis all the time. He should be here now, to help this poor child. But where he is? In America, with he nose stick-up inside that white-woman crotch."

There. Every time something go wrong, Judith always bring up Luther. The man leave five years now but, for Judith, he come like a ghost in the house causing trouble. Jason switch off his ears, leave her on one end of the counter and went to the next end, by the medicine cupboard.

He fish out the Panadol. "I giving him this and some juice," he say.

Judith nod, but she staring like her mind far.

"You want me stay home from school? I could stay with him, if you want."

Judith nod again, but with a small smile that make Jason feel better. "Tell him I coming now," she say. "Lemme finish with these sandwich."

It feel like a long time Jason sit down on the bed, patting Kevin, before Judith reach and shoo him. She hug Kevin, tell him not to give Jason no trouble for the day, promise him she coming home early and she carrying him doctor tomorrow. Jason leave them and went to feed Growley, change his newspaper—stink of piss—and full his water bowl.

By the time Judith come back out, she had on work clothes

and the seven o'clock news did start. "Don't let him bathe," she say, eyeing the TV. "Just a li'l sponge-off around ten. And if he don't want the corn beef, make a pack-soup."

"I know, Mammy," Jason say, resting down his cornflakes and milk. "Is not like is the first time. Don't worry, nah."

"Hush," Judith lift she hand like a policewoman. "Turn up the volume, there."

Police clash with a Jamaat down Rio Claro. The reporter show a clip of a round-face black fella, with Muslim topee and tunic, riling up a crowd. JOSEPH X: COMMUNITY LEADER, the writing on the TV say. The fella had a Yankee twang, saying words like "oppression" and "discrimination" and "retaliation" and making them sound so highfalutin and nice.

She point to the TV and say, "Steups. Them black-Muslim-and-them is the worse. Always jihad-this and jihad-that. Police should shoot they ass. A setta bloody criminal, twisting religion to cover they bullshit."

Jason insides start twinging-up. He picture what Judith woulda do if she know he going by Pleasantview masjid this morning.

She grab she handbag and continue complaining out the door. "I working for Dr. Hosein donkey-years and I never yet hear him talk hard. You know how much patients does can't pay and he does tell them is okay? He does live good with everybody, not like them li'l black boy who feel you must step off the pavement for them, because they wearing long beard and long tunic."

Jason close the door fast, fast behind Judith. Then he run across by the couch, just to make sure it had no Datsun 280C waiting downstairs this morning—Judith did claim she break up with Selwyn, she man-friend, last week. That fool used to walk in here like he build the place, shouting and calling Jason "boy" and telling him "bring this . . . bring that." Who the hell Selwyn did feel he was?

Jason stay there a li'l while, shifting from knee to knee on the couch, watching through the louvres, waiting for Judith to get in a taxi. If she did only look up behind her, she woulda catch him, and she mighta think he being overprotective. But Jason did just want to make sure she gone.

He bathe fast and put on his school clothes ("Always wear uniform," Parlour Man did say. "Less suspicious, nah.") Jason peep in the bedroom to make sure Kevin still sleeping. He rip a page from his notebook and write: I COMING BACK NOW. He leave it on the kitchen table, weigh down by the bottle of peanut butter.

In the parlour, it only had a lady buying newspapers, so Jason didn't have to wait long for Parlour Man attention.

"Morning," he say, unzipping his Spiderman lunch kit. He put it on the counter, near the semicircle gap in the burglar proof where Parlour Man serve people. "Two juice and a aloo pie, please." That's what Jason was supposed to say every time.

Parlour Man chuckle. "Is okay, son. Nobody here."

The lunch kit disappear, then come back all zip-up again, only a li'l heavier.

"Remember your thing in there too, eh." Parlour Man say. "Don't forget to take it out before you give them the bag. You want a snack? Here." Parlour Man throw two pack of chocolate wafer on the counter. Jason did prefer vanilla, but he didn't want no problems with Parlour Man, so he take the chocolate and ride out.

As he step out the parlour, Jason two eyes meet and make four with Silence, the big boss of Lost Boyz gang. Across the road, Silence stand up in his gallery in boxer shorts and a wife-beater vest, and Jason had the feeling the man been watching the parlour for a while. Jason pores get bumpy like pineapple skin so he wave and walk off fast as possible. He didn't even know if Silence wave back.

In the room behind the masjid, Jason give the lunch kit to the Muslim man and watch him take out a white plastic bag, the kind Judith use home for garbage. *Lawd-a-mercy!* She would shred up his backside if she know he in here dealing with a black-Muslim. She could talk big, but Judith couldn't even give Jason "allowance" like them other children in school. Why he should feel bad about getting it somewhere else? A thing he hate was how, on Saturdays, Judith always come by the jooking board while he scrubbing the neck of his school shirts, just to remind him, "Take it easy, eh. I still paying the Chinee for them thing." Like he was a burden to she.

The man swing the lunch kit by the strap and Jason catch it, light and empty now. Last week, the thing in the plastic was brick-shape and so heavy Jason corn beef sandwich did get squash. The man dip in the pocket of his tunic and pull out a blue hundred dollar. He had it pinch between two fingers when he say, "Here, Small Man."

"Thank you, sir," Jason say, reaching for the money, but he end-up grabbing air because the man flick the note away.

"Next week, somebody important want to meet you," the man say.

"Yes, sir." Jason wonder who it is he talking 'bout. The word "important" make him remember the Yankee fella on the news. But all that wonderment get wash 'way when Jason grip the money.

In two steps, he bounce out the door feeling happy like pappy. Two guards—boys looking li'l older than him—was waiting outside the room to walk him back to the masjid gate.

"Wha' yuh smilin' so for, Smallest?" one boy ask Jason.

"Nothing, nothing," he answer. This hundred, combine with the hundred Parlour Man did give him earlier, combine with the two hundred he did earn last week—his first week on the job— mean he was just one delivery away from the Jordan sneakers he wanted so bad.

He wish he didn't have to go back home to see 'bout Kevin. He wish he coulda head straight in school and tell Shaka he get through with another successful mission. Few weeks ago, it was Shaka who did pull Jason aside after football and ask him if he interested in a li'l hustle. For a Form Three fella with moustache-and-thing to notice him like that, Jason did feel kinda special. "Easy money," Shaka did say, "How you think I end-up with a Nintendo and three different Jordan? Clean money, too. All you doing is toting a bag. Police can't lock you up for that."

Jason had to admit, as he walk back home, the money didn't feel so clean, but it feel real good anyway. He wasn't hurting nobody. He wasn't in no gang. He was just helping out his-own-self, that's all.

The next week, it had a different man in the back room. Although a white topee cover-up most of his head, on the sides, hair like dirty sheep wool—a kinda blondish brown—was curling out. The fella face was white as a white-man but he had a nigger nose and nigger lips, and that same curly hair make a bleach-out afro on his jawline. The weirdest thing, though, was the man eyes—so light brown they was almost orange—darting and flickering like two mini flambeau.

The man rest his palm on the desk and say, "Gimme the bag nah, boy."

Jason thief some more glances as he push the bag over. He never yet see a white Muslim, all the ones walking 'round Pleasantview was either black or Indian. Or maybe this man was some kinda albino, like the lady in the choir at Pleasantview RC Church where Jason went.

The man re-zip the bag but he keep his hand on it, the same way Growley does claim a toy bone.

"Sit down," the man say, and Jason follow because he couldn't do nothing else.

"You frighten I tell you sit down?"

"No, sir," he lie.

"What's your name?"

"Jason, sir."

"And your title?"

"Archibald, sir. I's Jason Archibald."

"*Humph*. Brother Younis really say you's a respectful fella. How much years you have, Jason?"

"Twelve, sir."

"Most fellas your age mighta shit they pants by now."

"I ain't frighten."

"You ever look inside the plastic bag?"

"No, sir."

"How come? You not curious?"

"Sir, excuse, ahhmm . . ." Jason swallow the crapaud in his throat and continue, "if I could just get the thing, please. I go be late for school, nah."

"Ain't school does start 8:30? You have a good half-an-hour still. Jason, I different from Brother Younis. I hadda know 'bout you before I give you my money."

Jason wanted to get away from this pushy, weird-looking man, but he wanted the money more, so he stay there answering plenty questions, all the usual ones grown-ups does ask children they now meet: where he living, with who, how much brother and sister he have, what subjects he like in school.

At long last, the man smile and slide the lunch kit across. He wave a small fold of money, the blues on top covering the purples, the greys, the greens and reds.

Jason watch them blues like how thief does watch mango on a tree.

The man peel one off and put it on the desk, "For today," he say. Then he peel off a next one and rest it on top the first. He move quick—*Voosh*—and push the money across the desk like is something for Jason to sign. "Come li'l earlier, next week. Seven. *I* go be here, not Younis."

Jason grab them bills. He shove them in the pocket of his uniform pants to meet-up with what Parlour Man did pay him earlier. Finally, he had enough for the new Jordans. He had more than enough.

"Yes, sir. Seven o'clock," Jason say, jumping out the chair so fast it skate on the floor tiles.

"Wait," the man say, when Jason almost by the door, "I's Brother Omar. No more "Sir," okay?" The man stand up, and he was real tall, he had to bend to pass through the arch doorway behind the desk.

As usual, them guard boys flank Jason as he step down from the room and march him out.

Two zebra crossing later, Jason stroll in the schoolyard in time for Assembly. Lining up in the courtyard, Shaka see Jason and use his eyebrows to pitch the question: *How it went?* Jason reply with a big-man nod—the kind that go chin up instead of down—but he really wanted to jump and wave the three hundred dollars warming his leg. More "allowance", he figure, than any other boy in the history of Pleasantview Government Secondary School.

Saturday morning, Jason didn't even care how fishy he look. He wake extra early, finish his most important chore—scrubbing the bathroom—then he ask Judith if he could go Pleasantview Junction to meet Shaka.

"For what? I done tell you: my blood don't take that boy. He have a sneakiness 'bout him." She was stripping off the sheet-and-them because Kevin did pee-down again. He wasn't a hundred percent better but at least he was eating solid food—cereal—and watching cartoons in the living room.

"Nah, Shaka is a cool fella, Mammy—he just quiet," Jason say. "W'happen, the Form Fives had a raffle and two-ah-we win Sneaker King vouchers, nah. We going early—soon as they open—to choose a shoes."

"A-A that remind me," Judith say, dumping the sheets in the washing machine, "your father send some shoes and jersey for allyuh. It by your grandmother. Since you going out the road, is best you pass for it before you go Sneaker King. Next thing: you waste your voucher and end up with two same sneakers."

"Steups. You know Daddy is a shithound. He does only send a setta cheap, cheap 'I Love New York' jersey, and a setta fake sneakers mark 'Adidas' but with four stripe instead of three. I passing by Granny *after* I buy my thing."

"Awright," Judith say, wringing the washing machine knob 'round and 'round—too much times—like she distracted.

"Well, I gone," Jason say. Behind him, water start to gush.

"Ahhmm . . . Selwyn coming tonight," Judith say, over the water.

He spin 'round. She back was half-turn while she cutting open a pack of Breeze detergent like is surgery she concentrating on.

"I thought allyuh vex," Jason say. "I though I say he wring-up your hand the other day, and you not taking no shit from him that you ain't take from Daddy."

Judith start sprinkling Breeze like mad in the water. "Well, is Selwyn who carry me and Kev by the doctor. Is he who pay and is he buy medicine. The man might be a jackass but at least he's a willing fella, he does try to help me out."

"I don't want him here!" Jason bawl.

Judith slam the machine lid and face him. "Boy, catch your damn self. You bringing a cent inside here? You paying any bill? No! But you tellin' me who I could bring in here? Ha, Lord! Just move from in front my face. That's why I's can't stand you sometimes, you know. You does look just like your father and you does get-on just like him. He leave and gone but does still want to call and police my nanni. He fast-and-outta-place. And you worse!" She try to shoulder past Jason but he was taller and, probably, stronger. He make one push and she fall back against the machine.

In a way, the push feel real good—like something he did want to do long, long time—but in a next way, it frighten him that he could manhandle his own mother so. And the look on Judith face, too: how she eye get wide, wide and then small, small as she start to get up. He see when she watch the mopstick. He know she woulda beat him like a Good Friday bobolee, and he know he woulda fight she back this time. He didn't want to hurt his mother.

So Jason run out the house.

Straight down the steps and down the street, but when he reach the main road he stop running and start walking. No taxi—he just keep walking. Why she had to say he just like his father? In fact, no, it good she come out and say it plain. Now he know why she always vex with him for no reason. But if Luther so bad, why she stick-up on a man worser than Luther? If it hadda be so, why she didn't go by Selwyn house when his wife not there? If Judith only know how hard it was to fall asleep them nights, with all the giggling and the noises coming from her bedroom. Them nights, Jason used to feel like mashing-up something. That's what happen just now: he didn't mean to push her, but he just trip-off. He didn't mean it. He wish he could love his mother like when he was little, but she wasn't making sense to him no more; he done outgrow everything she had to say 'bout everything—especially Selwyn.

Jason start to feel tired and like he want to cry, but when he watch 'round, he done reach Pleasantview Junction. He slow down, pull out his rag, wipe his face and neck. His heart keep racing, though, and he feel it wouldn't stop. But, across the road, Shaka was standing up outside Sneaker King.

Jason breathe in deep then breathe out long and slow, like he strangling off his home-self. Then, he put on his school-self—the cock lip, confident one Shaka accustom with. They bounce knuckles and went inside the store. Jason wasn't sure if was the cold air blasting when they push the door or the big wall with so much pretty sneakers, but he feel a cool calm coming over him. Or maybe the coldness was inside him?

As he and Shaka went shoe by shoe along the wall, Jason take the opportunity to ask 'bout Brother Omar. Shaka say the man does only be interested in special fellas—the real intelligent ones, like he and Jason.

"Don't study how he look. That man teach me plenty important things," Shaka say.

"Like what?" Jason say. He point to a Air Jordan on the wall—red, black and white—and Shaka take it down.

"You's a li'l boy," Shaka say. "You ain't ready to learn them things yet."

Well, now-self Jason get interested. "Tell me, nah?" he beg, while the two of them examine the shoe.

"Sur-vi-val," Shakka whisper, and then he talk normal, "I real like this one—what size you's wear?"

The masking tape on the sole say size 7, 8 and 10 was in stock. Jason call for a 7 and start taking off his old shoe.

Shaka say, "And we does learn to protect weself." He put two fingers and a thumb like a gun, and point it at the Syrian lady reading papers behind the cash register counter. "We learn 'bout all these fuckers with light, light skin. Them is mutants."

That make Jason buss out a laugh. He realize Shaka wasn't serious; he was just playing the ass—like always.

Same time, the sales clerk reach back. The shoe fit real good.

"I go take it," Jason say.

By the cashier, while Jason counting the money, Shaka pipe up again, "Suppose your mother notice the new shoes, boy?"

That make Jason pause. Not because of the sneakers—Judith did buy that raffle story wholesale. No, was because of what she did say: he can't pay for nothing and that's why she need Selwyn. This six hundred dollars coulda help out Judith. But then, Jason remember how she say he fast-and-outta-place just like his father. Well, since she done cast him so, as wotless, it didn't make no sense trying to show she better. Let Judith haul she tail.

He push the money over the counter.

Shaka say, "Wear the thing now, nah?" but Jason say, "No, I hadda go down by my Granny. I fraid them fellas 'round there." Then he and Shaka part ways.

The fellas on the block wasn't the only reason he hate going by his father mother. She smoke too much and her husband had a rumshop downstairs and a setta drunk people was always there—Jason didn't like that. But mostly he didn't like seeing his Aunty Gail—everybody in Pleasantview know she was mad and everybody know what did send she mad.

Jason was little when the thing did happen, but he know the story by heart: how Aunty Gail was with a Syrian marrid-man and how he make she loss a child and how she thief a gun from Granny Janice husband and shoot the Syrian man. That was the last time Jason see Luther: five years ago, when Aunty Gail was in jail and he did come from America to meet the lawyers-and-them. He last one month, then Judith find out 'bout the American white-woman—the lady did call the house. Jason and Kevin was on the couch, peeping through the louvres, when Judith run Luther, "And don't fuckin' come back here!" The way Luther turn and watch them, Jason did know right then they loss they father forever. So he did buss out crying, but when Kevin start crying too, Jason had to force his own self to hush-up and be a good example.

The first time you do something so hard, it does stick in the back of your mind.

Seeing Aunty Gail always remind Jason of that bad day.

He reach Granny Janice house and shout from downstairs till she look out.

"Mammy send me for something," he say.

In two-twos she throw down a parcel and say, "Your father say call him when you get it."

"Yeah," Jason mumble, digging in the bag and finding the same kinda shit he did expect. He say, "Bye," and walk off. Couple years back, he and Kev woulda be so excited for these gifts from America—Kev was still so—but Jason know better now. Shit for shit—that's how Luther see them.

Jason rather dead than call that man and say thanks.

"Why you don't join we Youth Group?" Brother Omar ask Jason. "Kings of the Earth—the boys pick the name. We does meet Saturdays 'round ten. Come, nah?"

Jason did come early just like Brother Omar say, and he did done handover the lunch kit, and Brother Omar did ask him 'bout his weekend, and Jason did mean to only tell him 'bout the shoes but then he end-up telling his whole life story. Brother Omar had a way of listening, like you was the onliest person in the world and he didn't have nothing more important to do than hear you. But now, outta nowhere, he put Jason on the spot with this youth group question.

"Nah," Jason say, drawing out the word till he find a good excuse. "I's a Catholic, you know."

"That ain't nothing. You believe in Jesus?"

"Yeah."

"We too. Abraham, Moses, Mary . . . we believe. So what's the problem? Besides, you just tell me your father in America, your mother have a wotless marrid-man who does disrespect you. She brother—the teacher-fella—live with allyuh a li'l bit, but since he wife take him back he don't even fart on you. You need this youth group, Jason. You need wisdom and handlement. Plus, we does have real fun."

Like a wabeen fish out of canal water, Jason wriggle and squirm in the chair. He was starting to like Brother Omar, and the idea of having fellas to lime with every weekend sound cool.

But what to tell Judith?

"Listen," Brother Omar say, "You was frighten to wear your Jordan to walk down by your Granny, and you frighten to wear it to school. Trust me: if you was in Kings of the Earth, you coulda walk any street in Pleasantview. Nobody woulda dare touch you. People woulda cross the road when they see you coming. You know why? "

Jason shrug, wishing it had something to watch in this room, aside from the desk and the lonely picture on the wall— "the Kabah in Mecca," Brother Omar did call it.

"God does make the path of the disciplined man straight, Jason. Respect does precede him like a flaming sword. You don't want respect?"

Bam, bam, bam. Somebody knock the door and Jason feel glad for the interruption. Brother Omar say, "Come!" and one of the guard boys stick-in they arm with two fold-up newspaper. Brother Omar point his lips at the door, so Jason get up and take the papers. He rest them on the desk and sit, hoping the youth group talk finish and the money coming next.

"So as I was saying . . . " Brother Omar unfold the papers and, when he glance down at The Express, he stop talking and stay with his mouth open. His face get red like the headline. He bend over the front page like he suddenly catch glaucoma. Then he flip, flip, flip and start reading something. He let the rest of the papers drop and he hold up a page and say, "This is what I now telling you, Jason. Watch this picture. You know this fella?"

A dead man in the street, eyes half-open and watching the camera, blood running out his mouth. Anybody in Pleasantview woulda recognize him.

"Nah! They kill Silence? Which part it happen?" Jason bawl.

"In Town; Nelson Street. They ambush him. He shoot back the gunman though—a fella from Red Kings gang—the fella critical."

"Waaaaay," Jason say, shaking his head. He couldn't believe somebody could out Silence light so easy. One glance from him did give Jason goosebumps, the other day.

"Yeah. They did want him long time," Brother Omar say. "But notice it happen up in Town. Couple years ago, it mighta happen right outside your school. But gangland killing stop in Pleasantview. We in this Jamaat, *we* tell them it can't happen so again. *We* run things 'round here now, and them fellas could do their business as long as they keep peace in Pleasantview. I did watch Silence in his face and tell him, 'Boy, stop shittin' where you does eat.'"

"You coulda talk to Silence so?"

"Yeah, the man start right here, in this same Jamaat. In fact, I meet him inside here, five years ago. But the man didn't have no discipline in him. 'Islam' mean 'submission' and the man couldn't do that. I remain here in this family, he went with a next family—them Lost Boyz fellas. See how it end?" Brother Omar slap the page, then he say, "If a man hadda dead early, he must dead for something important. Not like this." He push the papers away. He wasn't red no more, he was whiter than usual, and Jason coulda swear it had a trembling in Brother Omar hand.

"Yeah, I sorry he end-up so," Jason say, trying to sympathize because the man seem real, real hurt 'bout Silence.

Brother Omar lean over the desk, latch his fingers and

watch Jason with them flambeau eyes. "Me and he . . . we was you. We didn't have no father. We didn't have no money, no setta education. It only had two road: he take one, I take the next one. Which one *you* want? Ask yourself that."

He open the top drawer and pass Jason two hundred dollars. "Come youth group this Saturday, nah?" he say.

Jason nod. "I will think 'bout it."

Brother Omar smile and both of them stand up and shake hand. When Jason try letting go, the man grip tighter and say, "Call your father like your Granny tell you, eh."

Jason rock back. "Why? To hear the same nancy story again? How he still fixing papers for me and Kevin to go America?"

Brother Omar squeeze even harder and say something Jason didn't understand, "Stay on him. A disciplined fella like you could do big, big things in America, walking quiet among them infidels."

Friday evening, Kevin was on the floor in front the TV, legs skin-out like a Peace sign, scribbling in his Hulk coloring book.

"Where Mammy?" Jason say, as he walk in and dump his knapsack, lunch kit and football gear.

"She gone by the Chinee grocery for bread," Kevin say.

Judith handbag was on the kitchen counter, as usual. Jason keep his back to Kevin, and move at a angle, so Kevin wouldn't see the blue note he slip inside Judith bag. Whole week Jason did feel worser and worser 'bout fighting with her.

By the time he bathe and come back out, she was there and getting ready to make dinner. Jason watch how she drop her wallet in the handbag and push it further down the counter. He wonder how long before she find the money. It didn't matter, though. Whenever she find it, at least *he* know it come from him.

"Evening, Mammy. Let me help you, nah," he say. He and she was talking again, but kinda cold still.

"Evening, Jay. Open them two tin of sardine for me."

Jason know he could convince Judith this first hundred was something she loss and find back. To really help out, though, he know he had to give more and make it look clean. Draining the fishy brine in the sink, he say, "I getting a small work. On Saturdays, nah. Is okay?"

Judith shrug. "I don't mind, once you finish your housework first."

Jason dump the sardines in a bowl and ask if he should cut up the onion and pimento. Judith say, "Yeah. But where this work is?"

"In Town. A sneakers store," he prattle off, his eye-them drilling hole in the cutting board. He shoulda think through this lie better. Suppose she ask the street or the store name? Suppose . . .

"Well, is high-time you pull your weight 'round here," Judith say. "I wukkin' since I thirteen. Anyway, your grandmother call. She say come tomorrow 'round ten. Me ain't know for what, so don't ask me."

Jason didn't intend to ask. He slice the last pepper and dash out the kitchen before the tide turn back to "work" talk.

In two-twos Judith fry the sardine, but when they sit down and open the sandwich loaf, a cockroach fly out the bag.

Kevin scream and Judith cuss like wind 'bout "them fuckin' nasty Chinee." Then she start ramfling through her bag for the receipt, so she could send Jason to change the bread. When she dip so, she pull out the hundred.

Judith raise she hand like she in church and bawl, "Oh-Lord-Father-Thank-You-Jesus! Where this come from? Me don't remember this."

Jason ain't say a word, but his chest puff-up till he had to whistle out the pride he feel.

Then Judith say, "That Selwyn, eh. Is *he* do this. I tell you, Jason, the man have bad ways, but a good heart."

The rage that fly up in Jason head make Judith face turn blurry. For years, *he* been the one helping her, minding Kevin and doing all the man-things in this house. She never yet say thanks. Is like she don't even see him. But she hurry, hurry to see the best in fuckin' Selwyn.

He grab the money and storm out. "Forget the stupid receipt," he say.

Granny Janice was standing up over Aunty Gail, with a length of cane in her hand—the kind people does weave basket with in the Blind Welfare Shop.

"She giving so much trouble to take she pills these days," Granny Janice say, "And the bitch bad like crab when she don't take them. I go call the mad-house, let them come for she. I tired of this shit."

Aunty Gail was crying but she put a pill in her mouth, real slow.

Jason remember Luther beating him with cane switch: every blow that miss used to make a *whoop* in the air, and every blow that land used to burn like jep-sting and leave a wale.

"Now drink some water," Granny Janice say. "Is running down marrid-man have you so: off your fuckin' rockers. If you did keep your leg-and-them closed, you woulda been good still."

Aunty Gail start crying louder. Jason couldn't understand why she never retaliate. Easy, easy, she could wrestle that whip from Granny Janice. But Aunty Gail always had this hang-dog, po'-me-one look, like she feel she suppose to get beat-up and cuss-up all the time, like she feel she deserve it.

"Alright, nah, Granny," Jason say, "she swallow it, so relax." He was in the recliner, trying to ignore the cigarette stink of the chair fabric.

The phone ring. Granny Janice say, "Answer it. Is quarter-past-ten. That must be your father." Then she drop the whip, say, "I goin' in the toilet," and speed off down the corridor.

Jason confuse. She did tell him he come to change curtains. He start cold-sweating but he couldn't think what to do, so he answer.

"He-e-e-y," Luther start in that American accent he pick-up since he gone New York. And, sure as the sun raise over Pleasantview every morning, he say all the things Jason know he woulda say. "Why you didn't call me, yo? Moms told me she gave you the message. Is it Judith? She didn't wanna buy you a phonecard or sumt'n? Anyway, you like the stuff? They fit? How you doing in school? How's Kevin? Remember: you his big bro. I'm getting my shit together with this paperwork so I can get you guys over here. I changed lawyers, that's all. Little setback."

Jason keep mumbling: mmm-hmm, ah-ha, yeah, good—and, still, the man never notice is cold-shoulder he getting. Luther just keep talking and talking like he fraid silence.

Then he say, "I got sumt'n to tell you, Jay. That's the reason I wanted to talk to you so bad. Nobody knows, not even my Moms—where she at? Can she hear what you sayin'?"

"Nah, she in the toilet," Jason say. He coulda tell Luther that he did hear another click, as if somebody pick up a next receiver. He coulda say that it had a strange, open-air sound to the call, too. But Jason wasn't sure if was Granny Janice to blame or the white-woman. He didn't want to cause no bacchanal.

"A'ight . . . well . . . here goes," Luther say. "You my firstborn. And I don't get to say it enough, but I miss you like crazy, son. I'm sayin': you got my heart, yo. Not that I don't love Kev—but you my first and that's a different kinda love. You feel me?'

Jason never yet hear his father talk so. And with every word Luther say, the boulder-size grudge on Jason chest get lighter and lighter—till he think he coulda stand up and bounce it like a beach ball. He couldn't totally forgive Luther yet—too much questions was in his mind still—but maybe he coulda start feeling a *few* good things for his father again. "Yeah, Daddy, I understand," he say.

"Good. You said 'Daddy' . . . I like that. So, yeah, certain things you deserve to know first. And, please, don't say nothin' to your Grandma or your mother or nobody, okay? I'll tell 'em when I'm ready."

"Yes, Daddy." Jason heart start a steelpan rhythm in his chest. *Lik-ki-ting-lik-ki-ting-lik-ki-ting* – that's all he was hearing. He figure Luther woulda say he coming Trinidad to spend a li'l time with them. Or better yet, maybe he buy two plane ticket for Jason and Kevin to finally go New York and see a "summer".

"Congratulations. You got a new baby sister," Luther say.

"What?" Jason hear a gasp but he wasn't sure if it was he who do it or the third person on the line.

"Yeah, Trinité Rebecca Archibald is one month old and she's beautiful, Jay. I can't wait for you to meet her. Maybe for Christmas I might—"

Jason drop the phone and he walk like a zombie straight to the center table and grab the cane switch. He watch Aunty Gail, she watch him, then she say, "Don't cry." With that, Jason take off running. He cross the gallery, he swing the gate and leave it skin-open, he run down the front steps, he reach the street and he just keep running. The new Jordans was on, but he run so hard his foot start to shock him. He cross the road running, he jump over drain and keep running. The whip was in his hand still, lashing the air with every stride, but sometimes it hit his ear too—and the lash feel better than what Luther did just tell him.

He loss his father again? Again?

He run straight through the masjid gate. The guards give chase, bawling, "Aye! Wait! Wait!" He run till he reach the room where Brother Omar does always be. He grab the door handle; it didn't turn, but he cling on and shake, shake, shake the door. The guards catch up; they scramble him and he start one big bawling and kicking and striking with the whip. He didn't have nowhere else to go! Why they couldn't understand that?

"Behave your fuckin' self!" one boy say. "Don't let we have to shoot you!"

"Leave him!" Brother Omar voice drop like thunder. The fellas dump Jason and he dump the whip. When he look behind him, Brother Omar stand up in the doorway of the small building nearby. "Come," he say, and Jason run to him.

Jason grab on to Brother Omar and cry. Loud, loud. Not like how a twelve-year-old suppose to cry, but like how Kevin does cry when he loss a race. Like he going and dead.

Brother Omar hold on, too. He kinda drag Jason inside and close the door. "Shhhh. W'happen, son?" he keep saying. When Jason calm down li'l bit, Brother Omar put him on a bench and take the one opposite—it didn't have no desk, no nothing between them. He hand Jason a kerchief and Jason sniffle through the story 'bout the phone call.

Then he sit down there, back bend and head low, twisting the kerchief till it resemble rope.

Brother Omar shake Jason knee and say, "Don't blame him. I did want to tell you that long time. Try understand the man situation: he in America. He in a vice-grip plenty stronger than him. You know what the Bible say 'bout America? Watch me."

He lift Jason chin, real gentle. That's when Jason notice the blackboard on the far wall. He could see, over Brother Omar shoulder, a drawing on the board—a real good one—of a handgun, with a setta arrow naming the parts-and-thing. So Shaka wasn't joking, then?

"Pay attention. This important," Brother Omar say. "The Bible say America is 'The Great Whore.' You ain't no baby; you know what a whore is. It say she's the 'Mother of Prostitutes', and that we, black men, the *true* kings of the earth, is doomed to fornicate with she and she stink daughters, till we don't know we-self again. That's the trap your father fall in, m'boy."

Jason eye did keep darting from Brother Omar face to the blackboard, squinting at them labels, until the moment Brother Omar did say "we, black men."

"But you not black," Jason say. Is something he did really want to ask the man long time.

"My mother black. But your question bring up my next point. I used to blame my father: How he could just leave? I used to study if something wrong with me, if is my fault the man run. But Islam teach me something: my father is a white-man—a predator—he born so. And look: your father gone and empty his-self inside a white-woman. No wonder he ain't the father you remember. You ever meet a white-person in real, son?"

Jason shake his head. "Only them Syrian-and-them," he say, remembering what Shaka did say in the shoe store 'bout light skin people.

"Them come like a branch of white," Brother Omar say with a nod.

Jason think 'bout Aunty Gail problems, and his father situation too. For the first time, he see the link plain, plain: white-people. "But I don't understand," he say. "Why them so different?"

"Listen some facts you never learn in school," Brother Omar say, his eyes lighting up. "In the beginning, it only had black people and Islam on earth. A man name Yaqub thought he was smarter than Allah, so he start experimenting to make a new setta people. He start messing with DNA, killing off dark skin babies, until he create a brown race. And he keep trying and trying, until after six hundred years he build a white race.

That's plenty years: lying and thiefing and murdering babies . . . all that evil get seep down inside them new bleach-out people. They born bad."

Jason change position on the bench and hug-up his knee. The whole thing sound like a sci-fi movie, but if Brother Omar half-white and he saying these things, then it had to be truth. That American white-woman: is she who fuck-up Luther, and is she who cause Judith to need Selwyn, so is she who thief everything from he and Kevin.

Brother Omar follow Jason and raise one foot on the bench. "Boy, that bad blood in me—in your half-sister too—it come like a curse. Like a holy war—a jihad—going on inside. You ever feel like that? But I thank Allah because it lead me to Islam. Sometimes, war does bring peace."

Jason watch the blackboard again and nod real slow. For five years, that's exactly how he did feel: like he warring inside. But right now, all his feelings was flat, and this flatness had him seeing straight and clean over his whole life. It wasn't scary and foggy no more. He was seeing a new road with black-and-white answers now. And that's all he did ever really want: answers, and to understand why things did happen to him the way they happen. Now, he feel free. He didn't have to be vex no more with his mother and father—it come like a weight he could finally put down. Now he had other people, the *real* culprit-and-them, to hate.

Brother Omar point to the blackboard. "Easiest thing to find in Pleasantview is a gun—check your aunt, she know that—so is best them boys learn 'bout it early. Tomorrow, I taking them in the bush, down Rio Claro, to practice. If they learn to handle that kinda power, they could do plenty good in this world. Plenty."

Jason pass back the handkerchief, but he couldn't see himself getting up and going home. For Judith to keep saying he wrong, he wrong? Nah, it feel better to remain here, with Brother Omar, on the side of rightness.

"I could come with allyuh, tomorrow?" he ask, feeling like *he* had flambeau eyes now.

"Of course," Brother Omar say, "As-Salaam-Alaikum . . . Brother Jason."

With that, he grab Jason neck and plant a kiss on his forehead.

Acknowledgments

THE STORIES IN THIS COLLECTION FIRST appeared in the following publications: "Six Months" in *The New England Review*; "White Envelope" in *Scarlet Leaf Review*; "Endangered Species" in *Kweli Journal*; "Loosed" in *Harpur Palate*; "Kings of the Earth" in *Epiphany*; "Santimanitay" in *LitMag*; and "The Dragon's Mouth (Bocas del Dragón) in *The Beloit Fiction Journal*.

I thank PEN America and Fernanda Dau Fisher and I acknowledge the following people for their unflagging support and encouragement: Hester Kaplan, Michael Lowenthal, Rachel Manley, Roslyn Carrington, and the Lesley University writers' community. Thank you to all who read and commented, thank you to Linda and Roger for their many sacrifices, and thank you to Sarai Ayesha for teaching me.

A native of Trinidad and Tobago, Celeste Mohammed graduated from Lesley University with an MFA in Creative Writing. Celeste's goal is to dispel all myths about island-life and island-people, and to highlight the points of intersection between Caribbean and North American interests.

Her work has appeared in *The New England Review*, *Litmag*, *Epiphany*, *The Rumpus*, among other places. She is the recipient of a 2018 PEN/Robert J. Dau Short Story Prize for Emerging Writers. She was also awarded the 2019 Virginia Woolf Award for Short Fiction, and the 2017 John D Gardner Memorial Prize. for Fiction.

She currently resides in Trinidad with her family.